The Beauty with Poison 1

——Listen to the Dragon's Roar

Shuang Chenyue

Published by Great Wall Publishing, 2024.

THE BEAUTY WITH POISON
First edition. May 28, 2024.

Written by Shuang Chenyue.

The Beauty with Poison

Volume One: Listen to the Dragon's Roar

Chapter One: Mistakenly on the Dragon's Bed

On a moonless, windy night, perfect for murder, the cold chirps of cicadas resound through the old trees.

Timothy Shaw didn't know who first said this, but he thought it perfectly described his current situation.

At this moment, Timothy stood before a pit in the ground. Inside the pit lay a man, head bleeding and face ashen, while Timothy, holding a shovel, was tirelessly scooping dirt into the pit.

The man's face in the pit was gradually being buried under thick layers of soil. From the beginning until now, Timothy hadn't dared to look into the pit. He was a bit superstitious and feared that the man might suddenly open his eyes while being buried.

"If you don't mess with me, I won't mess with you. You made the first move. I didn't want to kill you!"

Timothy gasped, wiping the sweat from his forehead as he spoke.

Yes, Timothy had never aspired to be a murderer. For eighteen years, though idle and lazy, he abided by the law and was a model citizen. Just six hours ago, while wandering the streets of Poiema, he couldn't have imagined he'd be burying a corpse in an unknown forest in the middle of the night.

Indeed, everything had started six hours ago.

Timothy was born and raised in Poiema, a true Poiema native. His family made a living selling perfumes and spices, owning a modest business that was enough to support them.

On this particular day, Timothy was wandering aimlessly in the street when an old man with a face full of wrinkles called out to him.

The old man scrutinized him from head to toe, sighing, "What a handsome young man, with such striking features."

The old man pulled Timothy aside and, after some questioning, learned that he was a local of Poiema, living an idle life at home.

The old man said, "I know a wealthy family plagued by misfortune recently. They consulted a sorcerer who said they need a young and handsome man to perform a ritual to ward off the bad luck. If Mr. Shaw is willing to come with me, there will be a generous reward."

Timothy loved money, and upon hearing of a generous reward, thought to himself, "How could I miss out on such an opportunity?" Without much thought, he readily agreed.

As it turned out, his greed led him to this predicament.

Timothy followed the old man into an alley and was ushered into a flower palanquin.

The palanquin had no windows, its sides sealed tightly, making it feel like a large, sealed box with only a thumb-sized hole at the top, allowing some light to filter in for ventilation.

This made Timothy uncomfortable. He wondered if this was how rich people behaved nowadays. It felt like he was treated more like an item than a guest.

Full of doubts, Timothy sat in the palanquin, swaying as it was carried for several miles before it finally stopped.

Thinking they had arrived, Timothy prepared to relax, but stepping out of the palanquin, he saw only another alley and a chest filled with clothes, with two tall guards standing by.

Bewildered, Timothy asked the old man, "Where is this?" The old man gave a cryptic reply, "Mr. Shaw, the next part of the journey will require some discomfort."

"What... hey!?" Timothy had no time to react before the guards grabbed him and stuffed him into the chest.

Finally sensing something was wrong, Timothy tried to protest, but a hand pressed him down, and the old man's voice came from above.

"Mr. Shaw, do not make a sound. We will arrive soon."

Timothy grumbled inwardly, wondering what kind of family would treat guests so bizarrely.

Having no other choice, Timothy resigned himself to fate, lying silently among the clothes like a fish on a chopping block.

After what felt like an eternity, the chest finally stopped.

"Mr. Shaw, you can come out now."

Relieved, Timothy climbed out of the chest, only to gasp at the sight before him. He found himself in a grand, luxuriously decorated mansion filled with exquisite porcelain and treasures he'd never seen before.

Soon, the old man entered with several servants and said, "Mr. Shaw, please bathe and change."

Timothy, stunned, asked, "Bathe and change??"

The old man, not wanting to waste time, urged, "The ritual is about to begin, Mr. Shaw, please hurry."

Several servants hurried Timothy into a side room. There, behind a screen, was a steaming bath filled with flower petals, and a burner emitting fragrant smoke that filled the room.

Without needing to lift a finger, Timothy was undressed and bathed by the servants, who even washed his hair.

Never in his life had Timothy been pampered like this. Any discomfort from the journey was quickly forgotten as he reveled in the luxurious service, thinking perhaps heaven wasn't much better than this.

But Timothy's bliss was short-lived.

After being washed and dressed in a sheer robe, he was led to a bed in another room.

"Isn't there supposed to be a ritual? Why are you taking me to a bed?" Timothy asked, puzzled.

The servants exchanged nervous glances, remaining silent. From their evasive eyes, Timothy sensed fear and a faint trace of pity.

No one answered Timothy's question, so he sat on the edge of the bed, full of doubts.

As night fell, he heard a series of light footsteps. Moments later, he saw a shadow cast by candlelight outside the window, lingering in front of the door as if hesitating. After a while, there was a creak as the door was gently pushed open, and a figure swiftly slipped inside, closing the door behind them.

The figure was slender, dressed in a yellow silk robe, with hair tied up high, appearing to be a young man. He pressed his forehead against the door, remaining silent with his back to Timothy for a moment before suddenly turning around.

Timothy was startled by the sudden movements of the man. They stared at each other, wide-eyed.

In the candlelight, Timothy finally saw the man's face clearly.

The man had delicate eyebrows and long eyes, lips as red as vermilion, and skin as white as jade. He seemed to be in his early twenties, an extraordinarily handsome young man.

For some reason, the man stared at Timothy after entering, saying nothing for a long time. The eerie silence was unbearable for Timothy, and he couldn't help but ask, "Who are you?"

"You don't need to know."

The man replied stiffly and, as if gathering courage, walked towards Timothy with his head held high.

The man's aggressive demeanor made Timothy feel an ominous premonition. His heart pounded, and he instinctively retreated, "Hey, what do you want? Don't come any closer! Do you hear me!?"

Ignoring Timothy's warning, the man climbed onto the bed, grabbed Timothy's wrist, and forcibly pinned him down.

"From now on, I will fuck you," the man said, staring into Timothy's eyes, enunciating each word.

"... Fuck!?" Timothy was so shocked he almost choked.

Since the Harris family took over the Central Plains, renaming the country Great Alvah, fifty years had passed. And this delicate young man before him was none other than Christopher Harris, the third-generation emperor of Great Alvah.

Hearing this, Christopher became utterly enraged, his fair and refined face turning bright red. "Shut up! Right now, I'm the one fucking you. What's with your attitude? This is outrageous!"

"Fuck you! I came here because I heard someone needed a young man to ward off evil and was willing to pay. So, this whole time, it was just to sleep with me!? That's fraud! What, being the emperor means you can be shameless!?"

"You... you, a mere commoner, dare speak to me like this..." Christopher trembled with anger, clearly unprepared for Timothy's audacity, his face turning red and white in distress.

A brief exchange of words allowed Timothy to grasp his situation. His greed had led him to be lured into the palace, ending up on the emperor's bed by sheer coincidence.

Timothy couldn't understand why the emperor would use such underhanded methods to bring him into the palace. He only knew he was now facing the real danger of losing his chastity.

However, seeing the emperor, who seemed delicate and effeminate, getting flustered by a few harsh words, Timothy realized he was probably just a paper tiger, not as fearsome as he seemed.

In the end, it might not be his chastity that was at risk.

With this thought, Timothy felt more confident, leisurely watching him.

"So, Your Majesty, how do you plan to fuck this commoner?"

Perhaps not expecting Timothy to be so composed, Christopher shifted his gaze nervously, muttering, "Close your eyes. I... I don't like you looking at me like that."

What kind of look was that? Although Timothy wanted to ask, he instead playfully and seriously replied, "As you wish, Your Majesty," and obediently closed his eyes.

As his vision turned to darkness, the sound of breathing became clearer. The faint, fragrant breath lightly touched his face. Even without opening his eyes, Timothy could feel the other's nervousness.

He heard Christopher swallow, then felt a hand gently touch his cheek.

It was a hand that had never done hard labor, its soft and smooth skin clinging magnetically to his body, caressing from his face down to his neck and collarbone, then slipping into his thin robe, lovingly stroking Timothy's muscular chest and soft nipples.

Timothy's heart inexplicably sped up. The hand wandering over his body was too cautious, hesitating, yet the shy touches carried an undercurrent of long-repressed excitement. This hesitant foreplay only heightened Timothy's desire.

Suddenly, a soft, moist sensation landed on his chest. A nimble tongue circled his nipple, gently sucking, drawing sweet pleasure, making Timothy moan softly.

He opened his eyes to see Christopher, wholly absorbed, his head buried in Timothy's chest, licking and sucking with a dazed expression. From this angle, Timothy noticed Christopher's long, curled eyelashes fluttering like little fans, endearingly.

Was this truly the supreme emperor, the ruler of millions? If this was a dream, someone needed to wake him from this lascivious fantasy.

Unaware of Timothy's thoughts, Christopher continued to suckle Timothy's nipple, one hand involuntarily reaching between his own legs to caress his growing desire.

"Is it that tasty? It's been almost a quarter of an hour, and you still haven't had enough?" Timothy panted, his tone teasing.

"Shut up!" Christopher lifted his head, a flush coloring his eyes.

Timothy chuckled, "Your Majesty, you've been touching yourself for so long, are you unable to get it up?"

"Nonsense! You..." Christopher was both embarrassed and angry, unable to finish his sentence before feeling a sudden grip below. Timothy had boldly reached out and grabbed Christopher's desire.

"Ah—!"

Christopher let out an uncontrollable cry when his manhood was suddenly grabbed. Overwhelmed with shame and anger, he bit his lower lip and stammered, "What are you doing?! Let go!!"

Timothy held Christopher's not-so-impressive dragon root, examining it with feigned seriousness. "So this is the legendary dragon root? It's hard, but not exactly majestic. With this, you think you can fuck me?"

"Let go!!" Christopher shouted, tears of frustration welling up. "I told you to let go!!"

"A commoner won't let go, what can you do about it?" With that, Timothy flipped over, reversing their positions. In an instant, the situation turned upside down. Timothy, who had been lying obediently moments ago, now had Christopher pinned beneath him, pushing his way between Christopher's legs, forcing them wide apart.

"What... what are you going to do to me?!" Feeling the impending loss of his virtue, Christopher struggled desperately, his hands and feet flailing uselessly.

"With those skinny arms and legs, you think you can overpower me?" Timothy smirked, a roguish grin spreading across his face. He patted Christopher's delicate cheek. "Give up. Let me, no, let this commoner teach you what it means to fuck."

Chapter Two: Tragedy in Ecstasy

Christopher was struck like a bolt from the blue, watching Timothy shamelessly lower his head and take his dragon root into his mouth. Overwhelmed with shock and fear, Christopher pushed back frantically, only to find that his struggles excited Timothy even more. The sounds of Timothy's slurping grew louder.

Timothy was not only diligent with his mouth but also busy with his hands. While Christopher was reeling from the sensation, Timothy boldly ripped at his clothes. With the sound of fabric tearing, Christopher's pants were shredded.

The sudden coldness brought Christopher back to his senses. As a sovereign ruler, he had never encountered such audacity, nor suffered such indignity. He beat and shoved at Timothy's head, but his physical disparity and pampered upbringing left him weak against Timothy's robust strength. To Timothy, Christopher's resistance was mere flirtation, arousing him further.

"Stop... mmph!!"

Before Christopher could call out, Timothy stuffed a piece of torn pants into his mouth. He then used another piece to bind Christopher's delicate wrists to the bedhead.

"Mmph mmph...!"

Christopher's tears flowed freely, but he was helpless. He couldn't cry out or fight back, watching as Timothy spread his legs wide, exposing his most private parts.

In the candlelight, Timothy closely examined Christopher's private area. It was a pink, virginal slit, hidden shyly beneath his slender root. His pubic hair was sparse and light-colored.

Christopher's mix of shame, fear, and trembling only added to his allure. Timothy swallowed hard, "I've never tasted a man before. Your Majesty, forgive this commoner."

Christopher, unable to struggle anymore, heard Timothy's words and shook his head frantically, trying to shrink away. Timothy, however, was relentless, grabbing Christopher's waist and pulling him back. He positioned his own aroused member at Christopher's entrance.

Though Timothy knew about sexual matters, he lacked patience. Spitting into his palm, he smeared it on himself, then forcefully parted Christopher's legs and pushed his shaft in.

The unlubricated entry was excruciating for Christopher. His eyes widened, and he let out a piercing scream, but Timothy pressed on, forcing the large head halfway in. Christopher's body shook violently, tears streaming down, while Timothy, driven by pleasure, pushed forward, embedding himself fully into Christopher's depths.

The sudden, intense pain caused Christopher to faint, his body arching off the bed. Timothy, finally sheathed in the tight, untouched passage, felt a rush that nearly made him climax.

"Fucking a man feels incredible. I'd die happy right now!" Timothy exclaimed, thrusting fervently. Christopher's body swayed with each movement, his eyes vacant, no longer resisting as Timothy took him forcefully.

Timothy, losing control, rammed his hardened flesh into Christopher repeatedly. After nearly a hundred thrusts, he felt the slickness inside. Looking down, he saw a mix of blood and fluids. Christopher's virginity had been taken.

Knowing he had deflowered the emperor, Timothy felt a dark satisfaction. The mighty ruler, now beneath him, utterly dominated.

Driven by this realization, he leaned down, removing the cloth from Christopher's mouth, and kissed his swollen lips passionately. Christopher, initially lifeless, responded to the kiss, a strange feeling stirring within him.

Timothy's lips were hot and demanding. Lost in the intense kiss, Christopher felt himself slipping into a daze. When Timothy finally pulled away, a string of saliva connected their lips.

Their eyes met, and Christopher's heart pounded as he looked at Timothy, who was also breathing heavily, staring back at him. Christopher had a small beauty mark at the corner of his eye, which, under the candlelight, made him look even more alluring and captivating. Timothy's heart stirred, and he leaned in to gently kiss that tiny black mole. Christopher instinctively tried to turn his head to avoid it, but Timothy's thrusts made him freeze, unable to move.

Seeing that Christopher was completely subdued, Timothy's mischievous nature surged. He untied the knot at the bedhead and lifted Christopher, maintaining their intimate connection, and sat at the edge of the bed. Christopher faced the door, his upper body hanging off the bed, his wrists still bound and resting limply on Timothy's shoulders. His legs, meanwhile, wrapped tightly around Timothy's waist.

"Ah... ah...!!"

Timothy lifted Christopher up and then let him drop heavily, each descent driving his hard member deep into the softest part of Christopher's body, as if trying to pierce his abdomen.

"Slower, slower..." Christopher begged, his head shaking wildly in Timothy's embrace, but Timothy ignored his pleas. His large hands gripped Christopher's buttocks, spreading them wide so he could penetrate even deeper.

Soon, the room was filled with the sounds of their lovemaking and the scent of their mingled arousal. Christopher, despite biting his lower lip, couldn't suppress the moans escaping from his mouth.

With glazed eyes fixed on Timothy, Christopher asked, "What... is your name?"

Breathless from the exertion, Timothy replied, "Answering Your Majesty, this commoner... is named Timothy."

"Timothy... Timothy..."

As he softly called Timothy's name, Christopher bit his lip, his body responding involuntarily, moving in sync with Timothy's thrusts, as if he were enjoying it.

Seeing Christopher's reaction, Timothy lost control, his body drenched in sweat. He held Christopher tightly and whispered in his ear, "I never thought the mighty ruler of a nation would be such a little slut."

Instead of getting angry, Christopher moved his hips more vigorously and moaned louder.

"Yes, I'm a little slut... Timothy... Timothy... mmph...!!"

Seeing this, Timothy's animalistic instincts took over, and he quickened his pace, his grip on Christopher's waist tightening as he pounded into him. Christopher's eyes rolled back, his head thrown back, hair coming undone in disarray.

"Your Majesty, this commoner... is about to...!"

Christopher shook his head desperately, "No! Don't come inside!!"

Ignoring him, Timothy growled like a hungry wolf, lifting Christopher's slender body as he stood up, beginning the final stage of their coupling.

"No! Don't...!"

Christopher's cries were powerless against Timothy's fierce assault. Finally, as Timothy's relentless thrusts brought them both to climax, Christopher screamed, releasing his seed.

At the same time, Timothy filled Christopher with his own, spurting deep inside him. Christopher's body twitched uncontrollably, overflowing with semen, which dripped onto the floor beneath them.

Still not entirely sated, Timothy moved inside Christopher a few more times before collapsing beside him, utterly spent. Soon, a heavy drowsiness overtook him, and he fell into a deep sleep.

Timothy slept deeply, vaguely hearing whispers around him. However, he was too exhausted to make out the words, catching only fragments like "dispose" and "bury him."

After an unknown amount of time, Timothy suddenly felt difficulty breathing. Groggily opening his eyes, he realized he was in complete darkness, bound tightly within a burlap sack. His hands and feet were tied with rope, and someone nearby was digging with a shovel, filling a hole with dirt.

The fragmented conversation he heard earlier came back to him in a rush, and he jolted awake, filled with panic. Just a short while ago, he had been lying with Emperor Christopher. How had he ended up tied up, about to be buried alive?

Could it be that Christopher, enraged after being violated, decided to execute him to vent his anger?

Regret washed over Timothy. If he had known it would come to this, he wouldn't have followed the mysterious old man into the palace, nor would he have forced himself on Christopher. Surely, offering up his own virtue would have been better than losing his life.

But he wasn't ready to die. At eighteen, he still had so much life ahead of him, so many dreams yet to fulfill. He couldn't accept dying here, now.

Determined to survive, Timothy began to wriggle, inching away from the person digging the pit. He moved like a caterpillar, inching slowly but steadily.

After some time, his head suddenly struck a sharp rock, causing a jolt of pain. The rock had a sharp edge, and as Timothy moved against it, he felt the sack tear slightly.

Overjoyed, Timothy maneuvered his hands to the tear, rubbing the rope binding his wrists against the sharp edge, hoping to cut himself free.

Meanwhile, the person digging continued, oblivious to Timothy's movements. As Timothy frantically worked to free himself, the digger looked around, noticing the sack had moved. Thinking nothing of it, he grabbed the sack's corner to drag it back.

The sudden motion helped Timothy break the rope, and he was thrown into a deep pit. From above, the digger began shoveling dirt into the pit. Seizing the moment, Timothy quickly freed his feet, tore the sack apart, and burst free.

The person above was caught off guard, letting out a startled scream. Instinctively, they dropped the shovel and stumbled back a few steps, landing heavily on the ground.

Timothy seized the opportunity to scramble out of the pit, dirt-covered and desperate. He quickly grabbed the shovel. The person recovered and lunged at Timothy, trying to wrest the shovel from his grip. Timothy was not about to give up easily; the two engaged in a fierce struggle, exchanging blows and grappling with each other.

"Who are you? Why do you want to kill me? At least give me a reason!" Timothy shouted while fighting.

"Let go!!" The person cried out, wincing in pain as Timothy yanked on their ear. "The emperor wants you dead. You have to die, whether you want to or not!"

Timothy didn't know martial arts, and the person wasn't a skilled fighter either. They fought like wild beasts, pulling hair and biting ears in a brutal, primal battle. Timothy's survival instinct gave him an edge. Summoning a burst of strength, he delivered a powerful kick that sent the other person flying. Their head collided with the sharp rock that had saved Timothy earlier, striking a vital spot. Blood spurted out, and the person slumped against the rock, motionless.

Timothy cautiously approached, feeling for a pulse under the person's nose. Nothing.

He was horrified. He only wanted to survive, not to kill. Yet here was a dead body, the result of his desperate struggle. What now? Where was he, anyway? Timothy looked around, seeing the dark, eerie forest. In the distance, he glimpsed flickering lights. Taking a deep breath, he decided he had no choice. He dragged the body to the pit, picked up the shovel, and started burying it.

He hadn't been working long when he realized this might not be the right course of action. If he was outside the palace, burying the body here might go unnoticed. But if he was still within the palace grounds, how would he escape after killing someone?

His mind raced. Suddenly, he had an idea. He jumped into the pit, unearthed the body, and stripped off its clothes, putting them on himself.

Though the person was dead, their identity might still help him escape the palace.

Having buried the body, Timothy, now dressed in the dead man's clothes, left the scene, heading towards the lights.

As he approached a beautifully landscaped garden with pavilions and corridors, he encountered several people dressed similarly to him. Timothy kept his head down, avoiding eye contact, and hurried past them.

Perhaps because it was dark, no one noticed anything unusual about him.

Timothy sighed in relief. It seemed he was still in the palace. His disguise was helping him blend in. Without it, he would likely have been caught as an intruder.

"Damn that emperor. He enjoyed it so much, yet now he wants to kill me without a second thought," Timothy muttered under his breath as he walked. Suddenly, a group of people carrying a palanquin approached. Timothy quickly stepped aside, lowering his head.

As the palanquin neared, he smelled a strong fragrance. He didn't dare look up but heard a woman's voice from the palanquin, "Stop."

Chapter Three: The Human Seal

The palanquin halted. A richly dressed woman sat inside, turning slightly to observe Timothy standing stiffly by the side.

"You, what is your name?" The woman asked slowly.

Timothy froze. He had no idea what the dead man's name was. How could he respond?

"I... I..." Timothy stammered, then decided to gamble, "My name is Timothy."

"Timothy?" The woman frowned slightly. "A new eunuch?"

"Uh... yes! I just entered the palace today," Timothy quickly agreed.

A palace maid beside the woman snorted, "No wonder he doesn't know the rules. Seeing the Queen, he doesn't kneel, just stands there like a fool."

Timothy realized why the woman had noticed him. He immediately fell to his knees, repeatedly bowing his head. "I didn't know the rules. I deserve to die! Please, Your Majesty, forgive me!"

Initially, Timothy thought the woman was just a concubine. Little did he know, in Great Alvah's palace, only princes and the Queen were entitled to ride in a palanquin. A palanquin was essentially a luxurious chair carried by two or four bearers, depending on the rider's status.

Normally, princes and the Queen could only use a two-bearer palanquin. But this distinguished-looking woman was in a four-bearer palanquin, indicating her extraordinary status. She was none other than Queen Owen, the most powerful woman in Great Alvah.

"Alright, stand up," Queen Owen said, seemingly not angry. She leisurely leaned back in the palanquin, speaking slowly. "Come here, let me have a closer look."

Timothy stood and took a few steps towards Queen Owen, raising his head slightly.

Queen Owen examined his face closely, noting his sharp features and strong brows. She clicked her tongue in approval, "You're quite handsome. Whose eunuch are you?"

Timothy, sweating, made up a name on the spot. "Eunuch Cook."

"Eunuch Cook? The head of the kitchen, Remi Cook?" Queen Owen asked, raising an eyebrow.

Timothy quickly nodded, "Yes, that's right, Remi the Eunuch Cook!"

In truth, Timothy had no idea who Remi was. He had just guessed a common name and luckily got it right.

"Such a handsome young man, yet assigned to the kitchen. What a waste." Queen Owen shook her ornate fan, covering her mouth as she continued to study Timothy. "How about this? From now on, you will serve me."

Timothy was stunned, looking at Queen Owen in confusion.

All he wanted was to escape the palace. Why would he want to serve her?

"Why are you still standing there? The Queen has just promoted you. This is a great honor. Kneel and thank her!" The palace maid scolded sharply.

"Thank you, Your Majesty, for your great kindness. This servant... no, this slave obeys," Timothy said, kneeling and bowing gratefully.

"Move on," Queen Owen said, waving her fan and seemingly in a good mood after gaining a handsome and obedient servant by her side.

Timothy, with no choice but to follow, trailed behind the group. He had no idea where Queen Owen was heading. Glancing around, he saw the eunuchs and palace maids with stern, silent expressions, and he dared not ask any questions, fearing to invite more trouble by saying the wrong thing.

Following Queen Owen's palanquin, Timothy passed through several grand palace gates, finally arriving at a palace named Hall Zona. The palanquin was set down at the stone steps. Queen Owen extended her delicate hand and said, "Timothy."

Timothy quickly stepped forward, reaching out to take her hand. Queen Owen's face turned red with surprise, and the palace maid beside her immediately scolded him harshly, "How dare you touch the Queen with your dirty hands!"

Timothy, confused, replied, "My hands aren't dirty; I just washed them."

Queen Owen couldn't help but laugh at this and waved her hand dismissively, "Faith, let it go. This child just entered the palace and doesn't know the rules yet. Don't be too hard on him."

Faith, the palace maid, reluctantly held her tongue but shot Timothy a disdainful look.

Queen Owen placed her hand on Timothy's and gracefully descended from the palanquin. "You are quite straightforward and endearing, despite not knowing the rules. Come along," she said, smiling.

Queen Owen walked towards Hall Zona, her robes flowing behind her. Timothy glanced at Faith, who handed him a food box and whispered, "What are you standing there for? The Queen told you to follow. Didn't you hear?"

"Fine, I'm going," Timothy muttered, taking the food box. He thought to himself, "Who gave this lowly maid such a bad temper?"

"You...!" Faith started to retort but was met with a dismissive wave from Timothy as he turned and left, leaving her fuming and stomping her foot in frustration.

Timothy followed Queen Owen into Hall Zona, but the further they walked, the more uneasy he felt, a growing sense of foreboding.

When they finally entered the main hall, he understood the source of his unease. The place looked eerily familiar. Wait a minute... the decor, the layout, the bed—wasn't this where he and Christopher had been just moments ago?

Cold sweat broke out on Timothy's forehead. He had thought he had escaped the nightmare, only to find himself back where it all began. This cosmic joke was far from funny.

Unaware of Timothy's reaction, Queen Owen walked to an inner room where someone lay on a couch, back facing the door.

Naturally, it was the emperor of Great Alvah, Christopher, who had turned on Timothy after their tryst.

"Your Majesty, retiring so early tonight?" Queen Owen asked quietly from the doorway.

Timothy saw Christopher flinch slightly at her voice.

"I'm not feeling well today..." Christopher sat up, hugging his knees and looking pitiful.

Not feeling well, my foot! Timothy thought, recalling how Christopher had been moaning beneath him earlier. What an act!

Queen Owen approached, sitting beside Christopher. She placed a hand on his and said, "Shall I call the royal physician to check on you?"

Christopher jerked his hand away as if shocked, shaking his head vigorously, "No, no need. It's nothing serious. Just some rest will do."

Curiously, Christopher seemed fearful rather than affectionate towards his wife, Queen Owen.

Unfazed, Queen Owen retracted her hand, a cold smile playing on her lips. "Your health is paramount, as it concerns the state of the nation. Neglecting your health due to excessive indulgence could lead to dire consequences for the country. You must take better care of yourself, Your Majesty."

Christopher nodded meekly, "The Queen is right. I understand..."

"Timothy," Queen Owen called, "bring the food box and serve the emperor his supper."

Hearing Timothy's name, Christopher looked up, his face turning pale as he saw Timothy approaching with the food box. His eyes widened in fear.

"You..." Christopher instinctively recoiled, clutching the bedding.

Despite his own nervousness, Timothy maintained his composure better than Christopher. He opened the food box, taking out a bowl of sweet lotus seed soup.

Queen Owen noticed Christopher's odd reaction and narrowed her eyes, "What's wrong? Is something amiss?"

Christopher quickly shook his head, replying in a small voice, "No... nothing."

Strange, why didn't Christopher expose him? Timothy wondered but decided to go with it. He scooped a spoonful of soup and brought it to Christopher's lips. "Your Majesty, please, have a bite."

Christopher's expression and body language screamed reluctance, but under Queen Owen's watchful eye, he had no choice but to open his mouth, trembling.

The mighty emperor of Great Alvah, behaving like a frightened child in front of the Queen, was a sight to behold. Seeing

Christopher's discomfort, Timothy felt a twisted sense of satisfaction. He intentionally shoved the spoon in hard, making it clink against Christopher's teeth. Christopher yelped, covering his mouth and glaring at Timothy, eyes red and filled with tears. Queen Owen, oblivious to Timothy's mischief, sat back and watched as Christopher nervously finished the soup. She then took out an imperial edict, handing it to Timothy.

"Read it to the emperor," she commanded.

Timothy took the edict, noticing the bold black characters on the yellow scroll. He began reading aloud, "Central Palace has colluded with Grand Tutor Bowie Butler , deceiving the throne and conspiring in rebellion. They shall be deposed to appease the public..."

Christopher, clutching the bowl, listened in shock. By the time Timothy finished, he was trembling. The bowl fell from his hands, shattering on the floor as he knelt before Queen Owen, shaking his head. "This edict is a forgery! There's no plan to depose anyone! I... I had no idea!"

Queen Owen chuckled, fanning herself leisurely. "Why be so alarmed, Your Majesty? If I didn't trust you, would I present this edict to you personally?"

She stood gracefully and helped Christopher to his feet. "I know you were misled by slanderous words. Just tell me who advised you against me, and I'll overlook this as if it never happened."

Christopher hesitated, his gaze shifting, unable to decide. Queen Owen gripped his wrist tightly, her voice cold, "We were once husband and wife. I have always been loyal to you. These outsiders, no matter how persuasive, will always have ulterior motives. You must understand the importance of loyalty."

Faced with Queen Owen's relentless pressure, Christopher finally broke down. "It was... Secretary Robin Green... who advised me."

"And?" Queen Owen demanded.

"And...?" Christopher stammered, confused, another name slipping out, "And Chancellor Payton Simpson..."

Queen Owen's lips curled into a satisfied smile. She dragged Christopher to the desk, spreading a new edict before him and tossing a pen his way.

"Then sign this edict."

Christopher looked at the document, his face draining of color. "Execution of nine generations... isn't that too severe? Exile... can't that suffice?"

Queen Owen's eyes were sharp and unyielding. Christopher dared not protest further. Trembling, he picked up the brush and signed the edict.

Timothy watched in silence as the scene unfolded before him. His immense hatred for Christopher gradually faded, replaced by sympathy and pity. The image of Christopher signing the document with tear-filled eyes etched itself deeply into Timothy's mind.

Timothy understood that once Christopher signed his name, many heads would roll. Moreover, from the conversation between Christopher and Queen Owen, it was clear that Christopher was deeply loyal to these ministers. Yet, he was forced to sign a decree determining their fate, handing the sword to Queen Owen, allowing her to commence the slaughter.

When Christopher finally completed the document, the pen fell from his hand, clattering to the floor. He sat there, hollow and drained, staring blankly ahead.

Queen Owen took the decree, nodding in satisfaction.

Tears streamed down Christopher's face, and he closed his eyes, appearing as if he were ready to face execution.

Queen Owen laughed. "Your Majesty, look at you, crying over a few officials. Is it really worth it?"

She slipped the decree into her sleeve and turned to Timothy. "Timothy, accompany me back to the palace."

At her words, Christopher looked up in surprise, glancing between Queen Owen and Timothy.

Timothy quietly cleaned up the broken pieces of the porcelain bowl, replied with a "Yes," and carried the food box past Christopher.

As Timothy passed, he couldn't help but glance back at Christopher, who stared at him with tearful, bewildered eyes. The mix of despair, confusion, and emptiness in those eyes struck Timothy deeply. Even as Timothy followed Queen Owen's palanquin away from Hall Zona, those eyes remained imprinted in his mind, haunting him.

Chapter Four: The Emperor's Fate

The night was long and silent, a time when people usually drifted into sleep. Under normal circumstances, Timothy would have been in a deep slumber. But now, he stood in the cold wind, wide awake and counting the stars above out of sheer boredom.

It wasn't that he didn't want to rest; he simply couldn't.

After leaving Hall Zona, Queen Owen didn't return to the palace but headed straight to the Imperial Medical Bureau. As her personal attendant, Timothy couldn't leave without permission. Since Queen Owen didn't specify how long she would stay inside, Timothy had no choice but to wait.

Shortly after Queen Owen entered, sounds of scandalous behavior echoed from the Imperial Medical Bureau. More surprisingly, alongside Queen Owen's voice, there were several men's voices as well.

Initially, Timothy thought Queen Owen had come to the bureau for medical reasons. He hadn't expected her to engage in an orgy with the imperial physicians.

Timothy stood guard outside with a short, young attendant who looked a couple of years younger than him. Despite the shameless noises from inside, the young attendant remained as calm as a meditating monk.

Curious and bored, Timothy struck up a conversation.

"I'm Timothy, new to the palace. What's your name?"

"Sage Gray," the attendant replied without looking at him.

"Does the Queen... do this often?" Timothy pointed towards the Imperial Medical Bureau.

Sage looked at him, "Newcomer, in this palace, the less you know, the better."

Timothy chuckled, "For someone so young, you talk like an old man. But I admire your calmness in such a situation. Respect, brother, respect."

Sage sighed, "You serve the Queen now. In a month, you'll be as accustomed to this as I am."

It seemed Queen Owen's public debauchery was an open secret. By contrast, Christopher, alone in his vast chamber without even a maid to serve him, was pitiable.

Reflecting on how Christopher had brought him into the palace in such a secretive manner, Timothy found it all quite curious.

"But what about the emperor? Does he allow this under his nose?"

"Shh! Keep your voice down," Sage hissed, covering Timothy's mouth. "Do you have a death wish? The master's private matters aren't for slaves to discuss."

"I'm just curious," Timothy whispered back. "Doesn't it seem odd? The emperor is quite handsome and…"

"And what?" Sage eyed him.

Timothy swallowed the word "lustful" and said, "I can tell from his face that he's good in bed. So why would the Queen seek pleasure elsewhere?"

"You can read faces?" Sage asked skeptically. "Then you should see the emperor's face has a widow's peak."

"A widow's peak?!" Timothy gasped. "What does that mean?"

"It means you know only half the story," Sage replied. "There have been concubines and palace maids around the emperor, but none survived more than a year after being with him."

"Why?"

"Don't ask why. Just know it's fate," Sage said, clasping his hands in a prayer gesture.

Timothy, determined to get to the bottom of things, pressed on. "So, does the emperor have any children?"

"Only one," Sage whispered, glancing around before leaning closer. "The current Crown Prince's mother was a maid. She was the only woman who survived more than a year after being with the emperor but died the day after giving birth."

Timothy shivered. Whether or not Christopher was cursed, one thing was clear: had he not escaped earlier, he might have become another ghost in the palace.

Sage sighed, "Being the emperor isn't enviable. In this palace and even in court, the Queen has the final say. If the emperor had any spine or intelligence, he wouldn't be in such a pitiful state. But enough of this, I've said too much."

Timothy had thought Christopher wanted to kill him out of humiliation, but it was more complex. Christopher, isolated and weak, was nothing compared to the strong-willed and decisive Queen Owen.

The relationship between Christopher and Queen Owen was undoubtedly tangled. Why did everyone around Christopher die? Why did he secretly bring Timothy into the palace? Why didn't he expose Timothy to the Queen? The reasons were unclear, but they certainly went beyond mere superstition.

Despite Timothy's efforts to pry more information from Sage, the latter remained tight-lipped.

Queen Owen spent the entire night indulging herself in the Imperial Medical Bureau. At dawn, she emerged, glowing and satisfied, while the imperial physicians looked utterly drained, as if their life force had been sucked out. Timothy couldn't help but silently marvel at the scene.

When Queen Owen took Timothy's hand and flirted with him, he put on a composed face, afraid of getting into trouble. He no longer dared to touch her as casually as before.

Seeing Timothy resist, Queen Owen sighed, "Such a handsome young man, it's a pity you're a eunuch."

Timothy maintained his calm exterior, but inside he was relieved to have avoided her advances.

Though Queen Owen was indeed debauched, she was generous towards Timothy. She rewarded him with numerous gold and silver ornaments and added ten silver taels to his monthly stipend of 200 bushels of grain as pocket money. Nearly half of this money Timothy sent to his family outside the palace. To avoid arousing suspicion, he didn't disclose the full details of his palace employment, merely saying that a friend had helped him secure a job there, and his family didn't question it.

Inside the palace, Timothy was meticulous. First, he obtained the eunuch registry from the Department of Internal Affairs and secretly added his name, solidifying his identity and eliminating future worries. Secondly, he investigated the eunuch who had tried to bury him alive. After some inquiry, he learned that the unfortunate scapegoat was named Kamryn Hunter, a junior eunuch in charge of illness and death affairs, who had entered the palace less than a year ago.

Timothy forged a letter in Kamryn's handwriting, stating that he was leaving to mourn a family member's death, creating the illusion that Kamryn had left the palace.

Timothy wasn't sure if Christopher would see the letter, but he knew that even if Christopher suspected something, he couldn't openly investigate Kamryn's death. Kamryn was a low-ranking eunuch, and a thorough investigation might reveal that Christopher had lured men into the palace for his personal pleasure. How Queen Owen would react to such a revelation was unpredictable.

Since that night at Hall Zona, Timothy hadn't had a chance to see Christopher again. Honestly, Timothy still thought about

Christopher, mainly because of his physical attraction. After all, Christopher was the first man Timothy had slept with, leaving a deep impression. The memory of that night lingered in Timothy's mind, and he often wished for another encounter.

However, Christopher rarely left his quarters except for official duties. Though married in name, Christopher and Queen Owen led separate lives and rarely saw each other. As a eunuch in the Central Palace, Timothy couldn't wander to Hall Zona without reason. He pondered ways to see Christopher again.

Soon, an opportunity arose. Christopher was a devout Buddhist and visited Temple Lrisa in the forbidden garden on the fifth day of every month for a day of meditation and fasting, supposedly for spiritual cleansing.

This was the only day each month that Christopher left the palace. On these days, he would rise early, bathe in incense, and, accompanied by a few guards and attendants, spend the day at Temple Lrisa. It was also the day Queen Owen indulged herself the most, as Christopher's absence allowed her to freely engage with her lovers within the palace.

On the morning of the fifth, Timothy arrived early at Temple Lrisa. Soon after, Christopher's palanquin arrived, stopping at the temple entrance. Christopher stepped out, looking slightly thinner than before, with his delicate brows knit in a subtle expression of melancholy.

Dressed not in his imperial robes but in a simple, elegant dark blue ceremonial garment, Christopher exuded a serene and refined aura. He exchanged pleasantries with the abbot who had been waiting outside, then entered the temple with the abbot and a personal attendant.

Timothy had bribed the guards at the temple entrance, allowing him to slip inside unnoticed. Since Christopher disliked being disturbed during his meditations, only his personal attendant remained close, and the temple was otherwise quiet and serene, filled with the sounds of morning bells and birdsong.

In the northwest corner of Temple Lrisa was a secluded courtyard with an ancient tree whose massive branches extended beyond the walls. Christopher's attendant stood guard outside the courtyard, looking bored and sleepy. Timothy climbed over the courtyard wall, undetected.

As he landed silently in the courtyard, a familiar scent wafted through the air. Timothy couldn't recall where he had smelled it before but decided it didn't matter.

Timothy crept through the courtyard, approaching Christopher, who was kneeling and chanting softly before an altar, oblivious to Timothy's presence.

"Your Majesty," Timothy whispered into Christopher's ear, his breath warm against his skin.

Christopher jolted, turning sharply to face Timothy's close, smiling face. Startled, he dropped his wooden fish instrument with a clatter and instinctively moved to call for help.

Timothy quickly covered Christopher's mouth, pulling him into a tight embrace. "It's just you and me here, Your Majesty. Don't you remember me?" Timothy grinned.

Christopher trembled, nodding with wide, frightened eyes.

"Relax, I'm not here to kill you. See, I'm unarmed," Timothy said, guiding Christopher's hand over his chest and waist to show he carried no weapons.

Christopher blushed, quickly averting his gaze. "What... what do you mean, kill you? I don't understand."

"Come on, Your Majesty. There's no need to pretend. It's just us here. Don't you want to know how I survived that night?" Timothy asked, his smile turning mischievous.

Christopher's trembling eased, and he lowered his gaze. "Even if I knew, what difference would it make? I was a fool not to see that you were sent by the Queen."

"Sent by the Queen?" Timothy was puzzled.

Christopher, looking defeated, continued, "Never mind. At this point, what does it matter? Do what you must, but make it quick."

Timothy was taken aback. It seemed they were speaking past each other.

"Your Majesty, you're mistaken. I'm not the Queen's man," Timothy clarified.

Christopher looked up, bewildered. "What do you mean?"

Timothy released Christopher, adopting a serious tone. "I'm just an ordinary citizen. I have no connection to the palace whatsoever."

Timothy then recounted his background, how he was lured into the palace, and his encounter with Christopher, ending with, "If I lie about anything, may I be struck down by lightning."

"You really are an outsider?" Christopher murmured, "No wonder the Queen said nothing and left. I thought she brought you to confront me..."

"Confront you? About what?" Timothy asked, confused.

"I lured you into the palace behind the Queen's back, and she suspected something, so she sent you to test me."

Realization dawned on Timothy.

Christopher hadn't exposed Timothy's identity to the Queen because he thought Timothy was her spy. Admitting Timothy wasn't a eunuch would have revealed Christopher's actions outside the palace.

"Your Majesty, what's the deal between you and the Queen? Why are you so afraid of her? Why must you sneak around?

And what about the rumors that you bring misfortune to your wives—is that true?" Timothy pressed.

Christopher laughed bitterly. "Misfortune? That's just the Queen's excuse for silencing them."

"Silencing them?" Timothy echoed. "So, the palace maids and consorts who died... were they really killed by Queen Owen?"

Christopher gazed blankly into the courtyard. "I have no proof, but I'm certain it was her."

"Even the Crown Prince's mother?"

Pain flickered in Christopher's eyes. He gripped the door frame, his nails digging into the wood, leaving deep marks.

Chapter Five: A Forbidden Love

"The palace maid was my nightmare."

After a long silence, Christopher finally spoke.

"I had been married for many years, yet Queen Owen never bore me a child. She was intensely jealous and suspicious of any concubine or palace maid who got close to me. Anyone who shared my bed would soon die mysteriously. But as the emperor, I couldn't remain childless forever. Under pressure, Queen Owen chose a beautiful palace maid from her own attendants, blinded her, poisoned her vocal cords, and sent her to my bed, forcing me to... make love to her in front of her."

Timothy shuddered. "Blinded her and poisoned her voice? Why would she do that?"

"Isn't it obvious? She feared I would be drawn to the palace maid's eyes or voice. Can you imagine how I felt, forced to violate a helpless woman under the gaze of a devil? It was excruciating."

Tears streamed down Christopher's face as he spoke. The scene he described was too horrific to imagine. Timothy watched him, unable to find words to comfort him.

"If I could, I would erase that memory from my mind, but I can't. I still remember that night vividly..."

Recalling the past, Christopher trembled, hugging himself in fear.

"I was too frightened to perform, so there had to be a second time, a third time. It was unbearable for both the palace maid and me. We had no choice but to comply, repeatedly, under Queen Owen's watchful eye, until the palace maid became pregnant."

"But after she bore the prince, she was killed," Timothy sighed. Christopher turned to Timothy, his eyes filled with sorrow. "Since then, I've never wanted to touch a woman again."

Timothy crossed his arms, tilting his head. "So you turned your attention to men, finding them safer?"

"Compared to women, men are safer. At least, men can't get pregnant," Christopher said with a bitter smile. "But it doesn't matter. Queen Owen won't allow anyone close to me, regardless of gender. If she finds out, it won't end well for either of us. But, it was my idea to kill you to protect myself. It had nothing to do with anyone else."

Timothy shook his head. "You tried to kill me out of self-preservation, forced by Queen Owen."

Timothy thought he was being understanding, but Christopher's face grew more humiliated. "Are you pitying me?"

"Of course not," Timothy replied firmly. "I feel it's unfair for you. Queen Owen is despicable, flirting with her lovers while forcing you into a life of fear. She turned you into someone afraid of women! It's outrageous. Doesn't she fear retribution?"

Timothy grew more agitated, stepping forward to grab Christopher's hand. "Your Majesty, with me here, I won't let you suffer anymore."

Christopher, tears still on his cheeks, looked at Timothy in shock. "Do you mean that?"

"Though I'm just a lowly eunuch, I have my wits. Otherwise, I wouldn't have escaped death and be standing here talking to you, right?"

Christopher stared at Timothy silently for a long time, then suddenly broke down, sobbing in Timothy's arms. "For so many years, this is the first time I've heard such words..."

Timothy held Christopher's trembling body, gently stroking his back.

Christopher cried in Timothy's arms, his shoulders shaking. "Every word you said touched my heart. Even if it's a lie, I'm happy..."

"I wouldn't dare lie," Timothy joked, wiping Christopher's tears. "Lying to you would be a capital offense. My head would be the first to go."

Christopher looked up, his eyes wet with tears, studying Timothy's face. "Your head is too handsome to cut off."

Timothy's heart skipped a beat. He whispered in Christopher's ear, "Your Majesty, if you keep talking like that, I won't be able to control myself."

"Wh-what...?" Christopher stammered, unable to believe what he was hearing. "You... you missed me?"

"Ever since we parted at Hall Zona, I've wanted to see you again. But as a mere eunuch, how could I approach you? Do you know how long I've waited for this day?"

"I'm not a good person. I'm cowardly, weak, useless..." Christopher couldn't meet Timothy's eyes. "I'm selfish, despicable, heartless. I almost got you killed..."

"Look at me!" Timothy cupped Christopher's face, forcing him to meet his gaze. Christopher's body trembled, and the burning desire in Timothy's eyes reignited a spark in his heart.

"Your Majesty, I don't know what kind of person you are. But today, in this temple, I won't let you go."

With that, Timothy lifted Christopher and carried him to the bed by the window.

Christopher gasped in surprise, quickly covering his mouth.

Outside, the attendant named Rowan called out, "Your Majesty? Is everything alright?"

"Nothing! I'm fine!" Christopher quickly replied, trying to sound calm despite his breathlessness. "I want to rest in the temple. Stand guard outside and don't let anyone in."

"...Yes, Your Majesty."

Hearing this, Christopher relaxed slightly. His robe was already half-open, revealing his smooth, pale skin. Timothy leaned down, gently biting his collarbone, leaving a faint red mark.

To stifle his moans, Christopher bit his own hand, trembling under Timothy's touch.

Timothy's kisses traveled downwards, from his lips to his neck, as his hand slipped inside Christopher's robe, teasing his nipples. With his last bit of rationality, Christopher shook his head, gasping, "Not here..."

"Why not? There's no one here but us," Timothy murmured, sucking on Christopher's collarbone.

"No, Rowan is outside," Christopher blushed.

"Rowan?" Timothy realized. "You mean the one dozing off? Don't worry, he's probably sound asleep by now. He won't hear us."

"But..."

Christopher tried to protest, but Timothy silenced him with another deep kiss, leaving him breathless.

"Don't say 'but.' Your Majesty, do you know how long I've longed for you?" Timothy whispered.

"What...?" Christopher's eyes were misty. "You... longed for me?"

"Ever since we parted at Hall Zona, I've wanted to see you again. Do you know how long I've waited for this day?"

"I'm not a good person. I'm cowardly, weak, useless..." Christopher couldn't meet Timothy's eyes. "I'm selfish, despicable, heartless. I almost got you killed..."

"Look at me!" Timothy cupped Christopher's face, forcing him to meet his gaze. Christopher's body trembled, and the burning desire in Timothy's eyes reignited a spark in his heart.

"Your Majesty, I don't know what kind of person you are. But today, in this temple, I won't let you go."

With that, Timothy lifted Christopher and carried him to the bed by the window.

Christopher gasped in surprise, quickly covering his mouth.

Outside, the attendant named Rowan called out, "Your Majesty? Is everything alright?"

"Nothing! I'm fine!" Christopher quickly replied, trying to sound calm despite his breathlessness. "I want to rest in the temple. Stand guard outside and don't let anyone in."

"...Yes, Your Majesty."

Hearing this, Christopher relaxed slightly. His robe was already half-open, revealing his smooth, pale skin. Timothy leaned down, gently biting his collarbone, leaving a faint red mark.

To stifle his moans, Christopher bit his own hand, trembling under Timothy's touch.

Timothy's kisses traveled downwards, from his lips to his neck, as his hand slipped inside Christopher's robe, teasing his nipples. With his last bit of rationality, Christopher shook his head, gasping, "Not here..."

"Why not? There's no one here but us," Timothy murmured, sucking on Christopher's collarbone.

"No, Rowan is outside," Christopher blushed.

"Rowan?" Timothy realized. "You mean the one dozing off? Don't worry, he's probably sound asleep by now. He won't hear us."

"But..."

Christopher tried to protest, but Timothy silenced him with another deep kiss, leaving him breathless.

"Don't say 'but.' Your Majesty, do you know how long I've longed for you?" Timothy whispered.

"What...?" Christopher's eyes were misty. "You... longed for me?"

"Yes, ever since that night at Hall Zona, I've wanted to see you again. But as a mere eunuch, how could I approach you? Do you know how long I've waited for this day?"

"I'm not a good person. I'm cowardly, weak, useless..." Christopher couldn't meet Timothy's eyes. "I'm selfish, despicable, heartless. I almost got you killed..."

"Look at me!" Timothy cupped Christopher's face, forcing him to meet his gaze. Christopher's body trembled, and the burning desire in Timothy's eyes reignited a spark in his heart.

"Your Majesty, I don't know what kind of person you are. But today, in this temple, I won't let you go."

With that, Timothy lifted Christopher and carried him to the bed by the window.

Christopher gasped in surprise, quickly covering his mouth.

Outside, the attendant named Rowan called out, "Your Majesty? Is everything alright?"

"Nothing! I'm fine!" Christopher quickly replied, trying to sound calm despite his breathlessness. "I want to rest in the temple. Stand guard outside and don't let anyone in."

"...Yes, Your Majesty."

Upon hearing the response from outside, Christopher let out a sigh of relief. By now, the front of his deep robe had opened widely, revealing his pale, smooth skin underneath. Timothy leaned down, gently biting and nibbling on the small pink buds on Christopher's chest.

Christopher's robe was wide open, his soft black hair spilling over the bed. To stifle his moans, he bit his own hand, trembling delicately under Timothy's touch.

After a while, Timothy's hand slipped down, grasping Christopher's shyly erect member, stroking it gently. Tears glistened in Christopher's eyes as he emitted faint, barely audible gasps, his pitiable appearance greatly stimulating Timothy's desire.

"Ugh!"

When Timothy's fingers pried open Christopher's tight entrance and delved into the narrow passage, Christopher's eyes flew open in shock, his long legs instinctively clamping around Timothy's waist.

Recalling their first wild encounter, Christopher's face turned deathly pale. Timothy had taken him forcefully that first time, leaving Christopher's private parts torn and bleeding. Afraid of the scandal, Christopher hadn't sought help from the Imperial Physician, enduring a week of agony before finally healing. He could still remember the excruciating pain of those days.

Seeing Christopher's expression, Timothy knew exactly what he was afraid of.

"Don't be scared," Timothy murmured, kissing the corner of his eyes as gently as he could. "Last time, I was blinded by lust. This time, I'll be careful. I won't hurt you."

Timothy kept his word. This time, he was extremely patient. He started with one finger, then two, then three. He moistened Christopher's entrance with saliva, slowly increasing the number of fingers exploring the tight passage, gradually stretching it until it was wet and slick.

Simultaneously, he leaned down to take Christopher's member into his mouth, gently sucking and teasing it with his tongue. Under Timothy's dual assault, Christopher felt a pleasure he had never known. As Timothy pushed him to wave after wave of climax, Christopher instinctively clamped his long legs around Timothy's head, his body trembling as he released a thick, white fluid into Timothy's mouth.

"Your Majesty, are you satisfied with my service?" Timothy swallowed Christopher's essence, licked his lips, and looked up at him.

Half of Christopher's soul seemed to have drifted away. He murmured, "I thought I was going to die..."

Timothy chuckled, giving Christopher a light kiss on the lips. "Now, it's my turn."

With that, Timothy pulled Christopher up by the arm, flipping him over. Christopher knelt on the bed, hands gripping the windowsill, his bare upper body exposed to the sunlight.

"Don't...!" Christopher began to turn his head in panic, but before he could react, he felt a sudden pressure below. A searing hot member thrust into him without warning.

"Mmph!" The terror of that night resurfaced, and Christopher instinctively shook his head, his hands pushing helplessly against Timothy's body, but he couldn't stop the powerful intrusion.

"Why are you scared? Look, there's no blood this time." Timothy held Christopher close, soothing his trembling body while fondling his nipples.

Christopher's voice trembled, "I... I know... I just... ah!"

Before he could finish, Timothy gripped his waist and drove in deep.

"Don't blame me," Timothy whispered, biting Christopher's shoulder and taking a deep breath. "It's your fault. Seeing you like this, I just can't control myself."

With that, he thrust forward, nearly causing Christopher to collapse onto the bed.

Christopher bit his lip until it turned white, tears streaming down his face.

"Does it still hurt?" Timothy kissed the back of Christopher's neck, concerned.

"No..." Christopher shook his head, trying to suppress his voice. He turned his head and whispered, "Inside... it feels numb and tingly..."

Timothy knew Christopher was beginning to enjoy it. He stopped talking, grabbed his waist, and started moving slowly. Christopher braced one hand against the wall, the other covering his mouth, silently enduring Timothy's rhythm. The quiet temple echoed with their suppressed breaths and the creaking of the bed under their movements.

"Your Majesty? Are you really alright?"

Outside, Harlow seemed to hear something unusual and walked into the courtyard. Christopher froze, knowing that without the ancient tree's cover, his naked body would be visible to the attendant. But from Harlow's perspective, only a strand of Christopher's hair swayed by the window.

"Stay where you are!" Christopher ordered, his voice strained. Harlow stopped, not daring to move.

Timothy quickly pulled Christopher closer, pressing him against the wall while thrusting hard.

"Ah...!" Christopher let out an involuntary cry.

"Your Majesty?" Harlow looked worriedly at the window, now empty.

"There's nothing here for you. You can... leave..." Christopher managed to say while enduring Timothy's deep thrusts.

"Understood..." Harlow stood still for a moment, then reluctantly left.

Once Harlow was gone, Christopher sighed in relief. Without the prying eyes of the attendant, Timothy became bolder. He grabbed Christopher's arms and started thrusting vigorously, the sound of flesh meeting flesh echoing in the room.

Christopher, no longer holding back, matched Timothy's rhythm, moving his body freely. The temple filled with their passionate cries, each wave of pleasure more intense than the last.

"Right there... it itches..."

"Here? Or here?"

"Yes, there... harder..."

"Damn, Your Majesty, you're incredible..."

Their obscene dialogue continued as they switched positions repeatedly. Timothy released himself inside Christopher, on his face, and in his mouth, leaving him drenched in sweat and semen, utterly ravished. By the end, Christopher could only experience dry orgasms, his body convulsing in Timothy's arms until he fainted from exhaustion.

That day, Timothy and Christopher were like fire meeting tinder, igniting in uncontrollable passion. After Harlow left, they moved from the temple to the courtyard, from under the tree to the pavilion, from the wall to the pond. Whenever the mood struck, they indulged in their desires. Initially, Christopher was embarrassed, but he couldn't resist Timothy's persistence, eventually giving in and finding pleasure in it.

By the end of the day, even Timothy, known for his stamina, was exhausted.

But it was all Christopher's fault. He was like a drug, addictive and impossible to resist. Before meeting Christopher, Timothy never knew a man could be so intoxicating. Queen Owen wasted such a treasure, choosing other men instead.

As dawn approached, Timothy reluctantly prepared to leave. Christopher clung to him, unwilling to let go.

"You'll be gone for a whole month again," Christopher said, his heart completely captivated by Timothy.

Timothy didn't want to part with him either. He caressed Christopher's shoulder and said softly, "I'll find a way to see you back in the palace."

"But Queen Owen..." Christopher hesitated, fear in his eyes.

"I may be her attendant, but I'm not always by her side," Timothy reassured him, plucking a leaf from a branch near Christopher's face and blowing into it gently.

Christopher's eyes lit up. "What tune is that?"

"My family migrated from the southwest. My grandfather used to play this tune for me when I was little, so it's probably a folk song from that region."

"The southwest... what's it like there? I'd love to see it with you," Christopher said wistfully.

"We'll have the chance," Timothy promised, placing the leaf in Christopher's hand. "Whenever I miss you, I'll play this tune in the palace. When you hear it, you'll know I'm thinking of you."

Christopher carefully held the leaf, gazing at it before pressing it to his lips, a blush spreading across his cheeks.

Chapter Six: Deep Father-Son Bond

After returning to the palace, Timothy's mood was exceptionally good for several days, and he worked with double the enthusiasm. His colleagues couldn't help but ask if something good had happened to him. Timothy only replied that he had met an immortal a few days ago, who had given him a divination resulting in an extremely fortunate sign.

Sure enough, Timothy's diligent performance soon earned him a promotion to the manager of the Central Palace. This piqued everyone's curiosity, and many came to ask Timothy how he had encountered the immortal, hoping to share in his luck. The immortal, of course, was just a fabrication, but Timothy didn't disappoint them. To anyone who came to him, he gave a small sum of money for good luck. Gradually, Timothy's reputation for generosity spread throughout the palace, attracting more and more well-wishers and garnering him significant goodwill and influence.

Among Timothy's new acquaintances was a man named Blake Hunter, with whom he felt a special bond. Blake was from Galia, a year older than Timothy, and had the typical robust physique of a northern man. He had thick eyebrows and bright eyes, exuding a rugged yet refined charm.

Their first meeting occurred at the Eastern Palace. On that day, Timothy was sent by Queen Owen to serve as a reading companion. Crown Prince Vera Harris was playing chess with Vincent Butler, the son of Grand Tutor Bowie. Vincent, losing the game, secretly took several of Vera's white pieces. Vera noticed something amiss and accused Vincent of cheating, but Vincent denied it vehemently. Bowie, being Vincent's father and the Queen's brother-in-law, immediately sided with his son, accusing Vera of false allegations.

Bowie, with his powerful position, showed no respect for the Crown Prince, leaving Vera red-faced, angry, and tearful. Timothy, standing behind Vincent, had witnessed the cheating but, being of low rank, couldn't openly accuse him. Thinking quickly, Timothy shouted, "A mouse!"

Everyone was startled and looked towards Timothy, who pointed at Vincent's feet and exclaimed, "Young master, there's a mouse by your feet!"

Vincent screamed, nearly jumping in the air. Taking advantage of the chaos, Timothy grabbed Vincent by the collar, apologizing, "Excuse me," and shook him. To everyone's surprise, several white chess pieces fell from Vincent's clothes.

Blake, the Crown Prince's attendant, immediately spotted the pieces, picked them up, and demanded an explanation from Vincent. With the evidence clear, Vincent had no choice but to admit his wrongdoing. Bowie, thoroughly embarrassed, berated his son and left in disgrace.

"Mr. Shaw, we owe you today. Crown Prince, come thank Mr. Shaw," Blake said, lifting Vera in his arms and guiding his hand.

"Thank you, Mr. Shaw," Vera said, his eyes still glistening with tears but now shining with gratitude.

Timothy smiled, saying it was nothing, while inwardly noting how much Vera resembled Christopher—a true beauty in the making.

"But why doesn't the Emperor come if it's Eastern Palace readings?" Timothy couldn't help but ask.

Blake's expression darkened. "The Emperor... perhaps he still doesn't have the courage to face this child."

Timothy fell silent at these words.

"Prince Vera resembles his mother greatly," Blake said, gazing into Vera's large, watery eyes. "Especially his eyes. What the Emperor fears most is probably facing those eyes."

"But it's pitiful for the Crown Prince. Without the Emperor's support, people like Grand Tutor Bowie dare to bully him. Isn't that unfair?" Timothy remarked.

Blake shook his head. "You don't understand. Crown Prince Vera is known for his intelligence and kindness, admired by all. However, Queen Owen and Bowie's faction are so arrogant that they completely disregard him. Even King of Nixie once publicly rebuked Bowie for bullying the Crown Prince but was later accused by Bowie and exiled. If a straightforward and righteous King couldn't escape unscathed, we can't expect the Emperor to intervene."

"Blake, does my Imperial Father hate me?" Vera murmured, tugging at Blake's clothes.

"Of course not. The Emperor loves you more than anyone else in the world," Blake said gently, holding Vera's hand.

"Really?" Vera's eyes brightened as he turned to Timothy, "Brother Shaw, will you come visit me again?"

Timothy nodded firmly. "Of course!"

A gentleman's word is as good as gold. Having promised the Crown Prince, Timothy made a point to visit Vera and Blake at the Eastern Palace whenever he could.

Meanwhile, Christopher longed to see Timothy. As weeks passed without a glimpse of him, Christopher knew Timothy was busy with his new duties and didn't dare to seek him out, spending each night alone and restless.

One night, in the deep silence, Christopher had just lain down when he heard a familiar melody outside Hall Zona. Jolting awake, he hurriedly rose, donning only a thin robe and running barefoot outside.

Following the sound, Christopher reached a tree outside Hall Zona, but the music stopped. Confused, he looked around until Timothy leaped down from the tree, hugging him from behind.

"Got you, Your Majesty!"

Christopher gasped, turning in Timothy's arms.

"Why did you take so long? I've been waiting for you!" Unable to hold back, Christopher clung to Timothy's neck.

Timothy, moved and guilty, hugged Christopher's waist tightly.

"Forgive me, Your Majesty. I've been swamped with work. I barely found time tonight," Timothy said, kissing Christopher's lips. "Did you miss me that much?"

Christopher's body softened under Timothy's kiss, his voice trembling, "I did... day and night... I thought of you..."

Hearing this, Timothy couldn't hold back. He dragged Christopher to a corner, hastily untying his belt, "Your Majesty, I missed you too."

As Timothy's hand slipped inside, he found Christopher already wet and ready. Surprised, he smiled knowingly.

"Did you do this yourself?"

Blushing, Christopher bit his lip, "I thought you wouldn't come tonight..."

"Not just tonight, right?" Timothy teased, rubbing the tender flesh, "You must do this every night thinking of me."

"Mm..." Christopher moaned softly, "Who... who told you not to come..."

"You want it that badly?"

Timothy teased him, and Christopher couldn't help but cry out, "Yes... I want it..." He then pulled Timothy down, kissing him passionately.

With Christopher already prepared, Timothy wasted no time. He pressed his hard member into the slick opening, pushing Christopher against the wall.

Soon, the quiet night was filled with their gasps. Moonlight cast their entwined shadows on the palace walls, a silent witness to their forbidden passion.

Timothy thrust into Christopher against the wall, climaxing once, then lay down with Christopher straddling him, gripping his buttocks and thrusting into the wet heat again.

Under the moonlight, Timothy admired Christopher's disheveled yet seductive appearance as he rode him with wild abandon.

Christopher eventually looked down, gazing at Timothy with tender eyes. For some reason, Timothy was reminded of someone.

"Your Majesty, would you like to see the Crown Prince?" Timothy asked.

"The... Crown Prince?" Christopher paused, "Why... why bring this up?"

"The Crown Prince misses you. Every time he sees me, he asks when his Imperial Father will visit him."

Christopher fell silent, lost in thought.

Timothy shifted, pressing Christopher beneath him, kissing the delicate mole at the corner of his eye, and murmured softly, "Are you afraid?"

Unconsciously, Christopher's eyes reddened, shimmering with tears. "I... I'm ashamed of him... and his mother too..."

Blake was right. The guilt towards the mother and son was Christopher's biggest obstacle to meeting Vera.

"If that's the case, then you should go see him even more, shouldn't you?" Timothy whispered soothingly as he moved slowly, accompanying his words with gentle thrusts. "There's nothing to fear with me by your side."

Seemingly resentful, Christopher lay beneath Timothy, only emitting soft grunts without words.

Timothy thrust harder, catching Christopher off guard, eliciting a gasp from him. "Your Majesty, what's your answer?" His tone, though questioning, carried an undeniable authority.

Shaken by the thrust, Christopher's voice trembled as he responded, "Yes..."

"What was that? I didn't hear you," Timothy leaned closer, his ear near Christopher's lips.

"I... I promise you..." Christopher's voice quivered.

"That's right," Timothy smiled faintly, lowering his head to kiss Christopher's lips again.

Thereafter, they fell silent, consumed by fervent kisses beneath the swaying willows, entwined until the dewy grass below them was moistened by their passion.

The next day, Christopher kept his promise and accompanied Timothy to the Eastern Palace.

As they stepped out of the carriage, Christopher nervously grasped Timothy's hand. Timothy smiled reassuringly at him.

Christopher and Timothy walked side by side towards the entrance of the Eastern Palace. Before they could enter the courtyard, they heard a tinkling laughter.

"Blake, where are you?"

Vera stood in the courtyard, a blindfold covering his eyes, arms outstretched, playing hide-and-seek with the palace maids and eunuchs. Standing not far behind him was a tall man, silent but tenderly watching the crowd, unmistakably Blake.

Vera reached out with chubby hands, stumbling towards Christopher as if dizzy, only to trip over something and nearly fall. Christopher hurriedly stepped forward, catching him in his arms.

"I caught you!" Vera hugged Christopher tightly, giggling foolishly. "I know, you're Blake, right?"

Seeing Christopher's arrival, everyone quickly knelt down, not daring to breathe loudly.

Unperturbed, Vera remained oblivious, pulling off the blindfold from his eyes, only to be met with a face he had never seen before, leaving him momentarily stunned.

"Who are you?" Vera stared at Christopher with wide, watery eyes, bewildered.

Caught in Vera's gaze, Christopher felt an inexplicable warmth surging within him.

Despite his initial rejection of the Crown Prince before arriving at the Eastern Palace, every thought of him seemed to reopen a bloody wound in Christopher's heart. Especially upon hearing that the Crown Prince's eyes resembled those of his mother, Christopher inexplicably felt fear towards him.

Human preconceptions were peculiar indeed. Despite never meeting face to face, Christopher was convinced of his fear of those eyes.

Now, finally meeting the father and son, Christopher unexpectedly discovered the beauty of Vera's eyes.

Christopher knelt down slowly, gently caressing Vera's cheek. Countless words welled up within him, but he didn't know where to begin. Tears streamed down his face before he could speak.

Vera, astute as he was, seemed to understand something, and asked hesitantly, "Imperial Father?"

Unable to control himself any longer, Christopher hugged Vera tightly, sobbing uncontrollably.

"Imperial Father... don't cry..." Vera reached out, gently wiping away the tears from Christopher's eyes.

The scandal of Christopher being forced by Queen Owen to rape a palace maid and bear the Crown Prince had caused quite a stir in the palace. Especially among the palace maids and eunuchs serving the Eastern Palace, most felt sympathy towards Christopher and Vera's plight. Now, witnessing the father and son finally reunite, they couldn't help but be moved to tears.

Except for one person.

Blake stood nearby, expressionless, unmoved by the scene.

Timothy quietly approached Blake, whispering, "Blake, how can you remain unmoved by such a touching scene?"

Blake turned his head slowly, staring at Timothy for a while before finally uttering a few words, "I'm not Blake."

Timothy was taken aback, looking at him puzzled. "Not Blake? Then who are you?"

"I'm Arya Hunter. Blake is my brother," the man replied slowly.

Chapter Seven: Proximity

Later, Timothy couldn't help but marvel as he recounted the day's events to Blake and Arya.

"Blake, you're really not loyal! Why didn't you tell me you had a brother earlier?"

"Sorry, sorry. Arya is indeed my twin brother. So, what do you think? Aren't we quite alike?"

Blake put his arm around Arya's shoulder, and the two brothers stood side by side, making it hard for Timothy to tell who was who.

"Alike? You look like you were cast from the same mold."

Blake laughed heartily, "Even our parents often mix us up, let alone strangers."

Arya, standing silently with a stoic expression, was noticeably more reserved compared to his cheerful and outgoing brother.

"In fact, even the Crown Prince often calls me Arya and Arya, Blake."

At the mention of the Crown Prince, Blake's face softened with a paternal tenderness.

Timothy looked at him and suddenly felt compelled to ask, "Has the Emperor visited the Crown Prince since then?"

"To my knowledge, that was the only time." Blake sighed, his expression darkening. He turned to Arya, "And you, Arya? Have you seen the Emperor in the Eastern Palace since?"

Arya shook his head, "No."

"I can understand, though. If the Emperor frequently visited the Eastern Palace, Queen Owen would surely become suspicious. Who knows how she might torment the Crown Prince then?"

Blake seemed to be justifying Christopher, muttering to himself, "Speaking of Queen Owen, I've heard that her insatiable desires are no longer satisfied by the men in the palace. She's even started targeting those outside. Mr. Shaw, you're close to the Queen. Is there any truth to this?"

Timothy chuckled and leaned close to Blake, whispering, "To be honest, my friend, I am indeed responsible for that. Just recently, a new batch of fine goods arrived. Would you and Arya like to join me for a look?"

Blake's eyes widened with curiosity, "Can we?"

"Of course." Timothy nodded and turned to Arya, "How about you, Arya?"

Arya glared coldly at Timothy, furrowing his brow and crossing his arms, "Not interested."

Blake patted Arya on the shoulder and gave Timothy an awkward smile, "He's always been like this, not understanding the fun. You'll get used to it."

"Brother!" Arya grabbed Blake's arm, his voice deepening, "You shouldn't go either."

"This..." Blake looked at Timothy, then back at Arya, caught in a dilemma.

Sensing the tension, Timothy quickly intervened, laughing, "No worries, there will be plenty of opportunities in the future."

After bidding farewell to the Hunter brothers, Timothy left the palace alone and arrived at a villa named Terrace Torger in the western suburbs of Poiema.

On the surface, Terrace Torger was Queen Owen's private villa, but everyone in the Central Palace knew it was actually her love nest. Now that Queen Owen's faction controlled the court, men and women in the capital began to take advantage of their looks to gain favor, hoping to climb the social ladder by pleasing the Queen.

However, not everyone could catch the Queen's eye. Selecting suitable companions for her became a significant task. Since becoming the administrator, the responsibility of managing the palace attendants fell on Timothy's shoulders, including those at Terrace Torger. Though Timothy hadn't been in Queen Owen's service long, he quickly learned her tastes and preferences. The men he selected to present to the Queen always pleased her, earning him a reputation as a discerning judge.

Consequently, Timothy became a revered figure among the men at Terrace Torger. As soon as he entered the villa, a group of flamboyant men surrounded him, showering him with attention. Some even clung to his legs, calling him their benefactor.

Timothy visited Terrace Torger regularly under the guise of inspections, but it was mostly an escape for leisure. Here, away from the prying eyes of the palace, he enjoyed the attention and flattery of the beautiful men, chatting and relaxing.

However, one thing always bothered him.

"What's that smell? It's unbearable!"

Timothy lay back on a couch, frowning as the overpowering scent of perfume nearly made him faint.

"Master, wasn't it you who said the Queen loves men with a natural fragrance?"

A man knelt beside Timothy, peeling an orange and feeding him a segment with a soft, seductive voice.

"Ah, yes, that was my fault." Timothy slapped his forehead, remembering. He had indeed mentioned it casually once. Since then, the men started experimenting with various perfumes and oils, drenching themselves in fragrance.

They were used to the smell and didn't mind, but Timothy couldn't stand the mix of scents overwhelming his senses.

"Master," another man sidled up to Timothy, "Any decrees from the Queen today?"

"Decrees from the Queen..." Timothy chewed on the sweet orange, scanning the room. He suddenly remembered Queen Owen musing aloud during dinner the previous day, "Maybe it's time for something lighter and fresher."

"Lighter..." Timothy looked at the group of men, all overly made-up and garish. He realized there wasn't a single fresh-faced option among them.

With that thought, he sprang up and ordered, "Gather everyone. Roll call!"

Soon, all the men were assembled in the courtyard, lined up in rows. Timothy held a roster, standing on a platform, calling out names while scrutinizing each man.

He went through nearly the entire list, his initial excitement turning to disappointment.

When he called the last name, an eerie silence fell.

"Kalle."

"......"

No one answered.

Timothy called the name twice more, but still, no response.

"What's going on?" Timothy frowned at the roster, "Where is this person? Dead or alive?"

The men exchanged uneasy glances until someone in the corner spoke up, "Mr. Shaw, he's a cook. He should be in the woodshed."

"A cook?" Timothy's curiosity piqued, "Why is a cook's name on the palace roster?"

Another voice explained, "Mr. Shaw, Kalle sold himself to pay for his father's funeral. He agreed to do any work as long as he was paid, so he ended up working here as a cook."

Intrigued, Timothy decided to investigate.

"A cook who sold himself to pay for his father's funeral but only wanted to be a cook? Interesting. I'll go see him."

The woodshed was in the northwest corner of Terrace Torger, connected to the kitchen. Timothy rarely went there due to the strong smell of grease.

Kalle.

The name suggested beauty. Timothy wondered what the boy looked like. Being chosen to work at Terrace Torger, he couldn't be too bad.

Timothy was lost in thought as he stepped into the kitchen.

Suddenly, a dark shadow flew at his face. He didn't have time to dodge, and two sharp scratches burned across his cheeks.

A plump hen flapped its wings, slapping Timothy several times before feathers scattered everywhere.

"Ah! I'm so sorry!!!"

A shrill but clear voice sounded, and a boy rushed out of the kitchen, tackling the hen to the ground and gripping its legs tightly.

The boy, covered in dust, looked anxiously at Timothy, "Sir, are you alright?"

Timothy shook his head, dislodging the feathers, and looked up at the boy.

"Are you Kalle?" Timothy squinted, examining the youth.

The boy looked about fifteen or sixteen, with a round face and an innocent expression. His face was smudged with soot and grease.

"Yes!" The boy nodded, "And you are...?"

Timothy felt a bit disappointed, thinking that the boy was not particularly handsome, but since he was already there, he cleared his throat to break the awkwardness, "Why didn't you go to the courtyard when I called the roll?"

"Roll call?" Kalle was taken aback, then suddenly understood, "Oh! You must be Mr. Shaw!"

Kalle gave an embarrassed smile, scratching the back of his head, "I don't want to enter the palace. I'm fine just being a cook here."

Timothy deliberately put on a stern face, "Do you think you can just decide not to enter the palace? Is this Terrace Torger yours? Do you make the decisions here or do I?"

Hearing this, Kalle quickly shook his head, "No, no, that's not what I meant. I... I..."

Timothy watched him stammer for a long time, unable to form a coherent sentence, and felt even more disappointed. He thought to himself that such a clueless boy wouldn't last three days in the palace. With a heavy sigh, he turned to leave, muttering, "What's the use of you?"

"Mr. Shaw!!" Kalle suddenly rushed in front of Timothy and knelt down with a thud, "Mr. Shaw, please don't drive me away!"

Kalle thought Timothy's words meant he would be thrown out of Terrace Torger. Tears streamed down his face as he sobbed, "I lost my mother when I was very young, and my siblings all died of the plague. Recently, my bedridden father also passed away. To survive, I had to sell myself to bury my father. I've finally found a way to make a living here at Terrace Torger. If you drive me away, I might as well die right now!"

Timothy felt a wave of impatience; he hated it when people played the sympathy card. He was about to leave when he noticed the boy's face was blotched with black and white. It dawned on him that those blotches were dirt. Only then did Timothy realize that although Kalle was not particularly striking, his eyes were bright and lively.

His thoughts shifted, and he pulled Kalle up, saying, "Go wash your face."

"Huh...?" Kalle looked puzzled.

"Don't just stand there, go wash up!"

"Oh, oh! Right away!"

Kalle obediently ran into the kitchen, brought out a basin of water, and plunged his head in, scrubbing his face vigorously.

"Clean it well, not a speck of dirt left," Timothy instructed.

"Yes, sir!"

Kalle washed his face thoroughly until the clear water turned black. He finally lifted his head.

Timothy, seeing his face, was glad he hadn't left. He pulled out a handkerchief, tossed it to Kalle, then held the boy's head with one hand while rubbing his face with the other.

Kalle leaned against Timothy, bewildered, as Timothy scrubbed his face for a while before letting go.

Timothy tossed the handkerchief aside, pinched Kalle's cheek with a smile, "Now that's better."

Kalle, still confused, didn't realize that he now looked much more presentable, with clear features and bright eyes.

"With such a good-looking face, it's a waste for you to be stuck in the kitchen all day."

"But..." Kalle lowered his head, "I don't speak well, and I'm not very smart. Everyone says the Queen would never be interested in me. It's better for me to stay a cook."

"Is it up to them to decide whether the Queen will like you?" Timothy ruffled his hair, "In my opinion, you're better than those outside."

Kalle's eyes lit up, "Really?"

"But... the Queen doesn't just look at faces." Timothy crossed his arms, resting his chin on his hand, studying him, "Look at you, so skinny like a chick. Take off your clothes, let me see what you've got."

"Huh?" Kalle's eyes widened, "I have to take off my clothes?"

"Of course. What do you think the Queen summons you for? To listen to you sing or watch you jump rope?" Timothy leaned in close to Kalle's ear, whispering, "It's to enjoy your body."

"Body!?" Kalle was stunned.

"Enough talk, hurry up and strip."

"Okay..." Blushing, Kalle began to undress, piece by piece, in front of Timothy.

Chapter Eight: Sneaky Maneuvers

To be honest, Kalle's physique was unexpectedly impressive. Clothed, he appeared slender, but once undressed, his muscles became visible. Kalle often did heavy labor in the kitchen, such as chopping wood and carrying water, which inevitably built his muscles. The only drawback was that due to poor nutrition, his body was still somewhat thin.

However, what delighted Timothy the most wasn't Kalle's physique but the sight of his private parts. That thing, hanging limply between his legs, was shyly tucked in its foreskin, yet it was already a respectable size, certainly something Kalle could take pride in among his peers. Fully erect, it would surely bring Queen Owen immense pleasure.

"Mr. Shaw?" Kalle's voice trembled as he noticed Timothy staring at his crotch, "Can I put my clothes back on now?"

"Come with me." Timothy grabbed Kalle's hand and pulled him into the kitchen.

"Mr. Shaw!?" Kalle, confused, was about to ask questions when Timothy lifted him and placed him on the kitchen counter.

"Mr. Shaw..." Kalle's heart raced, and he cautiously asked, "What are you doing?"

"Training," Timothy smirked, gently grasping Kalle's soft member. "Judging by your condition, you've never touched yourself. This won't do for serving Queen Owen."

Unused to being held like this, Kalle's body trembled involuntarily. "Then...what should I...ah!"

Before Kalle could finish, Timothy had already started stroking him gently.

"First, you need to expose the head. It might hurt a bit at first, but don't worry, you'll get used to it."

As Timothy spoke, he carefully pulled back the tight foreskin.

"Ouch!!" Kalle's eyes filled with tears as he clung to Timothy's neck, shaking his head vigorously. "No, I can't serve the Queen like this..."

Timothy sighed, stopping his movements. He patted Kalle's back, "Whether you like it or not, every man goes through this. Otherwise, you can't be considered a true man. You're already this old, isn't it embarrassing to have your head still hidden?"

Kalle lowered his head and whispered, "But it hurts..."

Seeing that gentleness wasn't working, Timothy decided to take a tougher approach. His tone became stern, "Not willing? Fine, pack up and leave immediately!"

"No!" Kalle quickly looked up, desperately grabbing Timothy's hand, "Please, don't make me leave!"

After much hesitation, Kalle finally spread his legs obediently in front of Timothy, pleading, "Please don't make me leave. I'll listen to you."

"That's more like it." Timothy's anger turned to a smile.

Just as Timothy had predicted, Kalle's member was not only thick and long but also beautifully shaped. Under Timothy's patient strokes, it gradually became erect, the foreskin naturally retracting to reveal a smooth, round glans.

As it was his first time, the sensitive head caused Kalle to gasp and tremble uncontrollably. Though painful, there was an odd tingling sensation that made his lower abdomen twitch involuntarily.

"Mr. Shaw... my body feels... strange..." Kalle's voice was shaky, his legs squeezed together in discomfort. He tried to reach out and touch but was stopped by Timothy. By the time the foreskin was fully retracted, Kalle's member was standing upright against his abdomen.

Watching Kalle's arousal, Timothy himself was already fully erect. Unable to hold back any longer, he climbed onto the counter, pressing Kalle beneath him. One hand caressed the sensitive tip, while the other undid his own belt, freeing his erection to rub against Kalle's.

"Sir, yours is so big..." Kalle stared at Timothy's member, swallowing hard.

"Yours isn't small either." Timothy smiled, then pressed against Kalle and began to move.

The two rigid members rubbed together, each stimulating the other. It was Kalle's first intimate contact with another man's desire, and the overwhelming pleasure washed over him like a tidal wave. Instinctively, he began to move his hips, matching Timothy's rhythm, climbing to an indescribable peak.

Both Timothy and Kalle reached their climax almost simultaneously.

Kalle's first ejaculation left his mind blank, nearly causing him to faint from excitement. When he finally regained his senses, Timothy had already dressed neatly and stood before him.

"How was it? Wonderful, right?" Timothy helped Kalle up from the counter, wiping away his tears.

Kalle, still dazed, nodded, "It felt like I was floating in the clouds."

Timothy chuckled, "Wait until you serve the Queen; there will be even more delightful experiences. So, do you still want to stay here as a cook?"

Kalle's eyes widened, "Really? Will you be there too when I serve the Queen?"

Timothy shook his head, "Of course not. That's your task. I only train you."

Hearing this, Kalle's eyes dimmed slightly, "I see..."

Timothy thought Kalle was worried about serving the Queen and patted his head, "You have potential. I believe in you. Come, I'll dress you up properly and take you to meet the Queen."

Thus, under the envious and jealous gazes of others, Kalle was led out of Terrace Torger by Timothy.

Back at the palace, Timothy first let Kalle take a comfortable bath, then carefully selected an outfit for him and had the palace maids meticulously apply makeup.

By the time everything was ready, it was already night.

When the dressed-up Kalle appeared before Timothy, surrounded by the palace maids, even Timothy was surprised.

The boy in front of him had elegant eyebrows, rosy lips, and his loose robe revealed a hint of well-defined chest muscles. The belt was loosely tied, highlighting his slender waist. Kalle shyly lifted his eyes and nervously clutched his robe, "Mr. Shaw... do I look good like this?"

Timothy was momentarily speechless, finally nodding, "Of course, you look great!"

Kalle's eyes lit up, "Really?"

Timothy studied him for a moment, then frowned slightly.

"What's wrong?" Kalle asked, puzzled.

Timothy sighed, "I'm almost reluctant to let you go. It's like raising a cabbage just to have it eaten by someone else's pig."

Kalle tilted his head, "Someone else's pig?"

"Cough! Forget it, I didn't say anything." Timothy quickly grabbed Kalle's hand, "Let's go, I'll take you to see the Queen."

"Mr. Shaw..." Walking beside Timothy, Kalle looked up with innocent eyes, "The palace maids said that if I please the Queen, she might grant me a title. Is that true?"

Timothy nodded, "Yes, it's possible."

Kalle continued, "Then, if I become an official, can I work under you, Mr. Shaw?"

Timothy couldn't help but laugh, "You have such low aspirations. Others aim for high ranks, but you're content with being my subordinate."

"What's so great about being a high official?" Kalle pouted, "I'd rather stay by your side."

Timothy turned back, intrigued, "Why? What's so good about being with me?"

"Because you're a good person," Kalle said half-truthfully. "I can't explain it, but I just want to be with you."

Timothy chuckled, "Don't think too far ahead. With your wits, surviving in the palace is already an achievement."

As time would tell, Kalle not only survived but eventually became Queen Owen's most cherished favorite.

Chapter Eight: Sneaky Maneuvers

As Timothy had said, Kalle was different from the sycophantic favorites around Queen Owen. He lacked an obsession with power and status, and the innocence and purity in his eyes were qualities that the coquettish men of Terrace Torger did not possess. Queen Owen had seen many men but had never encountered someone like Kalle, making her favor him uniquely.

Timothy's keen eye for talent greatly pleased Queen Owen. Soon, he was promoted to Palace Manager. Thus, Timothy became the most important figure in the Central Palace, second only to Queen Owen herself.

One day, Queen Owen brought her trusted companions and favorites to the forbidden garden, hosting a grand banquet on a boat by the lake. Timothy and Kalle were among the guests. During the feast, Kalle remained by Queen Owen's side, peeling grapes and feeding them to her, occasionally refilling her favorite wine.

After several rounds of drinks and amidst the lively music, Queen Owen called Timothy to her side.

"Kalle is truly a handful," Queen Owen said, caressing Kalle's hand with a mix of helplessness and indulgence in her smile. "He insists that I give him a title."

Kalle's cheeks were flushed, seemingly a bit tipsy. He cautiously reminded, "Queen, you promised me..."

Queen Owen sighed, "I did promise, but your humble origins and illiteracy make it difficult. Timothy, what position do you think suits him?"

Timothy quickly replied, "Appointments are serious matters. I dare not make decisions lightly."

"Don't worry," Queen Owen waved dismissively. "I want your opinion. No one will blame you. Speak freely."

"Timothy..." Kalle's eyes were filled with eager anticipation.

Without needing to ask, Timothy knew Kalle hoped to work under him, but...was that really the best choice?

Staring into Kalle's innocent eyes, Timothy remained silent for a moment before finally speaking, "Queen, in my humble opinion, Kalle can be sent to the Eastern Palace to accompany the Crown Prince as his study companion."

Kalle was stunned, staring blankly at Timothy, unable to understand why he would say such a thing.

"Study companion in the Eastern Palace?" Queen Owen took a sip of her wine, her expression unreadable. "Why?"

Timothy respectfully replied, "Kalle is illiterate and can only do menial tasks. However, as someone close to the Queen, doing such work demeans his status and tarnishes the Queen's reputation. Yet, granting him a significant position could attract criticism and give ammunition to the Queen's adversaries in the court."

"Hmm..." Queen Owen nodded, "That's reasonable."

Kalle panicked upon hearing this, "But...!"

"Kalle." Timothy's stern voice immediately silenced him.

"Only by studying with the Crown Prince can you learn to read and achieve something in the future. Not everyone in the Great Alvah Palace has the privilege of being the Crown Prince's study companion. Don't be ungrateful."

Queen Owen also took Kalle's hand, "Kalle, Timothy's words are harsh but true. I've decided. From tomorrow, you will go to the Eastern Palace and study with the Crown Prince."

Kalle looked at Queen Owen and then at Timothy, realizing that the decision was final. He reluctantly agreed, but his spirit seemed deflated.

The next morning, Timothy arrived at the Central Palace to escort Kalle to the Eastern Palace as agreed. Kalle seemed to have had a restless night, with dark circles under his eyes, and remained silent and gloomy on the way. Finally, upon reaching the Hall of Eternal Joy in the Eastern Palace, he spoke, "Timothy, once I learn to read, can I stay with you?"

Timothy glanced at him, sighing, "You are so stubborn. Don't you realize that everything I said yesterday was for your own good?"

Kalle looked puzzled, "Kalle doesn't understand..."

Timothy, exasperated, said, "A wise bird chooses the tree it nests in, and a gentleman doesn't stay under a dangerous roof. Don't you understand?"

Seeing Kalle's blank look, Timothy slapped his forehead, "Of course, you don't know because you can't read. Just remember, the Crown Prince will be the future emperor. You must establish a good relationship with him."

Though Kalle didn't fully grasp Timothy's words, he nodded, "Oh..."

"Timothy~" A childish voice came from the garden of the Hall of Eternal Joy.

Before the voice finished, a small figure ran out of the hall and threw himself into Timothy's arms.

"You're here again! I haven't seen you for days!"

The person who leaped into Timothy's arms was none other than Crown Prince Vera.

Timothy hugged Vera, smiling, "Crown Prince! It's only been a month, and you've grown again! Let me see, hey, you're almost up to my waist!"

"Hehe!" Vera touched his nose proudly, "I've not only grown taller but also learned riding and archery with Arya. I'll show you later!... Huh?"

Noticing the stranger beside Timothy, Vera curiously examined Kalle and then asked Timothy, "Who is he?"

Kalle, startled, was nudged by Timothy and quickly knelt before Vera, "My name is Kalle. I'm the new study companion."

"Study companion?" Vera looked at him wide-eyed.

"Yes, Crown Prince. Kalle is new and knows nothing. You are his master now; please help him." Timothy interjected.

Vera, always kind-hearted, nodded vigorously, "Got it!"

He shook Kalle's hand enthusiastically, "Your name is Kalle, right? If you don't understand anything, just ask me!"

"Thank you, Crown Prince!" Kalle looked up, not expecting the esteemed Crown Prince to be so kind. His heart warmed, and the gloom on his face disappeared.

Chapter Nine: Concealed Pregnancy

Time flew by, and before anyone knew it, spring had arrived in full bloom. Everything in the Great Alvah Palace proceeded as usual, in an orderly fashion. Christopher and Queen Owen kept to themselves, avoiding conflict. Kalle, who was serving as a study companion in the Eastern Palace, was learning more words each day and had become the Crown Prince's close friend. Timothy continued his duties as Palace Manager, occasionally sneaking away to meet with Christopher, making life both busy and enjoyable.

Little did Timothy know, a storm was brewing beneath the surface of this seeming tranquility.

The first sign of trouble came when explosive news suddenly spread throughout the palace: Queen Owen was pregnant! The news caused an uproar. Everyone had long believed that the Emperor's lack of offspring was due to the Queen's infertility. Moreover, the strained relationship between the Emperor and the Queen meant that the Emperor had not spent the night in the Central Palace for a long time, and they had not shared marital relations for quite some time.

On the other hand, Queen Owen, believing herself to be infertile, had indulged in wanton behavior within the palace, reveling nightly with her favorites.

Now, the pressing question was: whose child was Queen Owen carrying? Rumors flew throughout the palace, and Kalle, who had recently become the Queen's favorite, found himself at the center of the scandal. Although Queen Owen insisted that the child was Christopher's and that she was carrying the imperial heir, everyone knew that the child's father could be anyone but Christopher.

Christopher learned of the Queen's pregnancy by accident while passing through the Imperial Garden, where he overheard palace maids gossiping. Shocked, he immediately summoned the maids and questioned them closely. The more he learned, the angrier he became, his face turning pale with rage. Such a significant event had been widely known throughout the palace, yet he, the supposed father, was the last to find out.

The Emperor of the nation, suddenly branded a cuckold, was enraged beyond measure. But what could he do? Queen Owen's faction held power and wielded it arrogantly, while he had no real authority. Even knowing the child was not his, Christopher could not take action against Queen Owen without damaging his own reputation. Resigned, he had no choice but to swallow this bitter pill.

In his frustration, Christopher questioned the maids about the child's father. They all hesitated but eventually named Kalle. It was only then that Christopher learned about the new favorite, Kalle, who was now studying in the Eastern Palace with the Crown Prince.

The man who had cuckolded him was now mingling with his son.

After much deliberation, Christopher decided to visit the Eastern Palace in secret to uncover the truth.

When Christopher arrived quietly at the Eastern Palace, Crown Prince's tutor, Mr. Robertson, was giving a lecture in the hall.

Crown Prince Vera sat upright at his desk, with Timothy standing behind him. Blake and Arya stood at either side of the hall. All eyes were on a young boy standing in the center, reciting poetry. The boy, dressed as a study companion, was about fifteen or sixteen, with delicate features and a modest height.

(Is that Kalle?) Christopher thought as he observed from a distance.

"In the garden, the amaranth is green, morning dew awaits the sun. Spring... spring..." Kalle stumbled over his recitation, struggling to remember the next line.

With a sharp crack, Mr. Robertson struck Kalle's buttocks with a ruler. "Spring nurtures all, everything flourishes in the light! You fool! Such a simple poem, and you still can't remember it after three days?!"

Kalle yelped, rubbing his sore backside, "My brain isn't good..."

"Dare to talk back?!" Mr. Robertson strode forward and slapped Kalle hard across the face.

Dazed by the blow, Kalle held his swollen cheek, staring blankly at Mr. Robertson.

"Mr. Robertson! Kalle has just begun to learn to read. He's a bit slow, but there's no need for such harsh punishment," Timothy said, stepping in front of Kalle protectively.

Mr. Robertson pointed at Kalle, his voice dripping with contempt, "Instead of striving to improve yourself, you seduce with your looks! You and your kind have turned our nation into a laughingstock! Ask around and see the rumors flying in the court. The honor of Great Alvah has been dragged through the mud by you wretches!"

Even Kalle, with his limited understanding, grasped the insult. Being called a seducer, a fox spirit—those words cut deeper than any physical blow.

Kalle bit his lip, his face pale, tears welling up in his eyes but not daring to fall.

"Mr. Robertson. Kalle didn't want to enter the palace. It was I who brought him here. If you must blame someone, blame me," Timothy said, shielding Kalle like a mother hen.

Christopher watched in stunned silence, (So it was Timothy who brought Kalle into the palace?)

Mr. Robertson, however, was unmoved. He glared at Timothy, "And you, Timothy, are no better! A mere sycophant who rose by currying favor with Queen Owen, a dog with a broken spine! You and your kind are why Great Alvah is in decline!"

"Mr. Robertson! You're wrong about Timothy!" Crown Prince Vera couldn't stay silent any longer. He ran to Timothy's side, "Timothy is always kind to me! Last time Vincent bullied me, it was Timothy who helped me. Please don't scold him."

"Your Highness..." Mr. Robertson was momentarily speechless.

"Indeed, Mr. Robertson," Blake added, "I was there too. Timothy exposed Vincent's theft and cleared the Crown Prince's name. Timothy may be a palace servant, but he's honest and loyal to the Crown Prince. I can vouch for that."

With both the Crown Prince and his aides defending Timothy, Mr. Robertson had no choice but to let the matter drop, announcing the end of the lesson and leaving in a huff.

Once Mr. Robertson left, Kalle finally breathed a sigh of relief and collapsed on the spot.

"Thank...you, Crown Prince," Kalle said, trembling as he bowed.

Vera shook his head, helping Kalle up. "Timothy saved you, not me."

"Thank you, Timothy..." Kalle started to kneel before Timothy, but Timothy quickly supported him, gently touching his swollen face, "Let me see how bad it is."

Kalle looked up, his tear-filled eyes pitifully fixed on Timothy.

"Your lip is split. Mr. Robertson didn't hold back," Timothy said, gently pressing his thumb to Kalle's lip. "Does it still hurt?"

Kalle nodded slightly, "It hurts..."

Timothy blew softly on his lip and smiled, "How about now?"

Kalle mumbled, "It's not the lip that hurts..." and pointed to his chest, "It's here."

Blake chuckled, "No wonder the Queen adores you, Kalle. It's been a while, and your skills at playing cute have improved. No man could resist, right, Arya?"

Arya replied indifferently, "Why ask me?"

Kalle blushed, muttering, "General Hunter is just teasing. The Queen doesn't only favor me." Then he looked at Timothy, "Timothy... that child isn't mine."

Timothy remained unmoved, "Oh? So?"

Kalle panicked, thinking Timothy didn't believe him, "It's true! I asked the Imperial Physician. The Queen's pregnancy is over three months along. I've only been here a little over a month. There's no way the child is mine!"

"Tall poppy syndrome," Timothy shrugged. "You're the Queen's favorite now. Don't you know how many people envy your position?"

"What's there to envy?" Kalle muttered, "I envy those who get to work under you."

Timothy placed his hand on Kalle's shoulder, patiently comforting him. Christopher, standing at a distance, watched everything unfold, feeling a pang of sadness before he turned and quietly left.

After leaving the Eastern Palace, Christopher remained despondent for several days. Even during court sessions with Queen Owen, he sat on the throne with a distracted and absent-minded demeanor. He seemed oblivious to the heated arguments between Queen Owen and the ministers happening right before him.

One day, during a court session, the virtuous officials led by Crown Prince's tutor Nathan Robertson clashed with Queen Owen. Nathan boldly exposed Queen Owen's indiscretions with her favorites and accused her of bearing a child by another man, thus plotting against the throne. Furious and humiliated, Queen Owen abruptly ended the court session.

After the session, Christopher and an enraged Queen Owen returned to Hall Zona. No sooner had they entered than Queen Owen began to curse.

"Nathan, that decrepit old dog! Does he think I'm a sick cat just because I haven't shown my claws?!"

She grabbed Christopher's hand and pushed him toward the desk, forcing a pen into his hand.

"Queen, what are you...?" Christopher looked at the blank decree in front of him, puzzled.

"Isn't it obvious?! You need to issue an imperial edict, declaring that the child is yours! Anyone who dares to speak ill of it will have their entire family executed! Let's see who dares to spread rumors and slander me after that!"

Christopher remained silent, his hand hovering in midair, unmoving.

"Write it!" Queen Owen demanded.

After a long silence, Christopher slowly put down the pen and stood up.

"I won't write it."

Queen Owen couldn't believe her ears: "What did you say?"

"I said, I won't write it." Christopher turned to her, his expression calm. "The child in your womb isn't mine, so why should I write it?"

"You...!" Queen Owen's face turned from red to white.

In a flash of fury, she pushed Christopher to the ground.

With a loud thud, Christopher's forehead struck the corner of the bed, drawing blood.

Dazed, Christopher saw stars and felt the world spinning. Before he could react, Queen Owen grabbed him by the collar and yanked him up.

"I address you as 'Your Majesty' out of courtesy. Do you think you have the right to defy me now?"

Christopher stared at the furious, almost unrecognizable woman before him, unable to comprehend what had driven her to such madness.

Queen Owen pinned Christopher to the ground.

"Someone get me the strongest liquor!"

"What are you doing?!" Christopher struggled under Queen Owen, realizing for the first time the terrifying strength she possessed.

Queen Owen held him down, calling out several more times before Timothy rushed in with a jug of liquor.

Seeing the scene, Timothy hurriedly pulled Queen Owen off Christopher.

"Queen, what are you doing?!"

Ignoring him, Queen Owen snatched the jug from Timothy, uncorked it, and began pouring the fiery liquid down Christopher's throat.

The liquor burned as it went down, choking Christopher, who thrashed and gasped for air, screaming for help: "No! Help...!!"

"Drink it!" Queen Owen forced more liquor into his mouth, "Tonight, you will issue that decree!"

"No... cough..." The liquor and tears streamed down Christopher's face as he choked and sobbed in desperation.

"Queen, you're mad!" Timothy shouted, finally managing to pull the crazed woman away from Christopher.

"Queen, if you don't care about yourself, at least care for the child you're carrying!"

Timothy's stern rebuke snapped Queen Owen out of her frenzy.

"The child..." Queen Owen collapsed into a chair, looking dazed. Suddenly, her face turned pale, and she clutched her abdomen in pain.

"Queen, what's wrong?" Timothy asked, alarmed, as he supported her.

"It hurts... my stomach... it hurts!" Queen Owen's forehead broke out in a sweat.

Timothy realized she might have disturbed the pregnancy. He shouted, "Someone, come quickly! The Queen is having pregnancy complications!"

A few palace maids rushed in. Timothy ordered, "Take the Queen to the Imperial Physician immediately!"

The maids hastily complied, carrying the groaning Queen Owen to the Imperial Medical Bureau.

Once everyone had left, Timothy rushed back to Christopher's side. Christopher lay on the ground, barely conscious, blood still oozing from his forehead. Timothy cradled his head in his lap, pinching his philtrum to wake him up.

After a while, Christopher slowly regained consciousness.

"Timothy... you're here..."

Tears welled up in Christopher's eyes as he saw Timothy, falling silently down his cheeks.

Timothy's heart ached at the sight. He pressed a clean cloth to Christopher's bleeding forehead and held his hand, "I'm here, I'm here."

Christopher looked at him with hollow eyes, "Am I a failure?"

Timothy gripped Christopher's hand tightly, shaking his head, "Your Majesty, don't think like that."

Christopher's tears flowed freely, "Don't comfort me. I know better than anyone. I used to think the problem was with the Queen, but now I realize it's me."

Saying this, Christopher was overcome with emotion, his breathing growing labored.

"Stop, Your Majesty," Timothy held him close, stroking his back, "Some things are beyond your control."

Leaning against Timothy's chest, Christopher gave a bitter laugh, "What good is being emperor? I can't father a child, can't openly be with the one I love, and can't even show affection freely."

Timothy understood the hidden meaning in Christopher's words. Each person had their own destiny, and Kalle had his own struggles and helplessness. But now was not the time for these discussions. Timothy held Christopher, offering comfort.

"Your Majesty, I won't stand by and do nothing," Timothy said in a low voice.

Today's events made Timothy realize that to save Christopher from this mire, Queen Owen had to be overthrown. But to do that, support from outside the palace was essential, as the corrupt officials alone wouldn't suffice.

Christopher, hearing this, clung to Timothy, tears streaming down, "Don't! She's a madwoman. She'll kill you. She really will!"

"Your Majesty, don't worry. I won't foolishly seek death," Timothy reassured him.

"Then what will you do?" Christopher looked at Timothy helplessly.

"Shh—" Timothy placed a finger on Christopher's lips, leaning in to whisper in his ear.

Christopher listened, becoming more agitated, shaking his head violently.

"I forbid it!"

"Your Majesty..." Timothy sighed.

"Please..." Christopher crawled up, wrapping his arms around Timothy's neck, pleading, "Don't go, I beg you..."

Without giving Timothy a chance to respond, Christopher pressed his lips to Timothy's, kissing him desperately. He thrust his tongue into Timothy's mouth, igniting a fervent passion between them.

When they finally broke apart, both were breathless. Christopher's eyes shone with a desperate, all-in resolve.

"You're all I have left."

Timothy's chest tightened with a surge of emotion, an intense impulse erupting from deep within. Unable to restrain himself any longer, he lunged forward, grabbing Christopher's body and kissing him fiercely. Christopher, equally lost in the moment, wrapped his arms around Timothy's neck and gently pulled him down, causing them both to collapse onto the bed.

The curtains fluttered, and the beaded drapes swayed as the two figures, entwined and enraptured, kissed passionately.

Meanwhile, just outside Hall Zona, Faith pressed her hand tightly over her mouth, her heart racing. She could hardly believe the shocking scene she had just witnessed. Timothy, the Queen's favored confidant, was entangled in such a relationship with Emperor Christopher.

It took Faith a few moments to recover from her shock. Realizing the gravity of what she had discovered, she quickly turned and hurried away to report the incident to Queen Owen.

"What?!" Queen Owen, who had just calmed down from her pregnancy pains, was stunned as she leaped up from her bed upon hearing Faith's report.

"Queen, please stay calm!" Faith urged, "You mustn't agitate yourself and risk harming the baby."

"Calm!? How can you expect me to stay calm after hearing this?" Queen Owen began to pace back and forth, deep in thought. After a moment, she turned to Faith, "Are you certain you saw and heard this with your own eyes and ears?"

Faith nodded vigorously, "I swear, everything I reported is the absolute truth."

Queen Owen's body began to tremble, "That Timothy! I have placed so much trust in him... and he dares, he dares...!"

Seeing an opportunity to stoke the flames, Faith added, "Queen, Timothy is undoubtedly still in Hall Zona! If we go there now, we can catch that treacherous man in the act!"

Queen Owen gritted her teeth, "Let's go! We'll head to Hall Zona immediately!"

Chapter Ten: Turning Crisis into Opportunity

When Queen Owen, accompanied by Faith, stormed to Hall Zona, the doors were tightly shut, and suggestive moans emanated from within.

"Your Majesty, is it here?"

"Yes, hmm... right here... yes! Harder..."

Faith wore a smug expression, confident in her discovery, while Queen Owen trembled with rage. She charged forward and kicked the door open.

"Timothy! You...!"

Her words faltered as she took in the scene before her.

Christopher lay on a couch, naked from the waist up, clutching a soft pillow, with a white silk cloth under his waist. Timothy, fully clothed, knelt beside him, hands pressed on Christopher's back, mimicking a massage.

"What are you... doing...?" Faith was equally stunned, utterly perplexed.

"Queen!" Timothy wiped sweat from his brow, raising his hands theatrically, "This is a new massage technique I recently learned from the Western Regions. It's said to be miraculous for relieving back pain and blocked meridians. The Emperor mentioned his shoulder pain and wanted to try it, so I humbly offered my services."

As he spoke, Timothy grabbed Christopher's ankle and bent his leg upwards, causing Christopher to howl in pain.

"Ah, it hurts! Timothy, be gentler... gentler..."

"My apologies, Your Majesty! But pain indicates a blockage. Enduring it will unblock the meridians."

"Timothy, you bastard! You're doing this on purpose! Ah—!!!"

Timothy pressed his palms together and quickly patted Christopher's back, then looked up at Queen Owen with an innocent smile.

"What's wrong, Queen? Do you wish to try it as well?"

"Uh... no, that won't be necessary..." Queen Owen took a step back uneasily, then whispered angrily to Faith, "What's going on!? You promised me a scandal!"

Faith, sweating profusely, stammered, "I swear I heard them..."

"Just this?" Queen Owen pointed at Christopher, writhing in pain under Timothy's hands. "You call this a scandal?"

Faith was at a loss for words.

"Queen, I swear I didn't lie. I also heard Timothy say he wouldn't stand by, and the Emperor called you a madwoman!"

"Really?" Timothy finally released Christopher and approached calmly, "Faith, if you dare to accuse someone, you must provide evidence."

Faith retreated, her voice shaking, "What... what evidence? I heard it myself!"

"Oh? So if you hear something, it counts as evidence? Does that mean anything I hear can be used as evidence too?"

"What nonsense are you spouting?" Faith shouted.

"Haven't you heard the rumor?" Timothy continued, picking up a sandalwood box and taking out a small sachet. "It's said a certain guard in Hall Zona carries a distinctive fragrance."

"A fragrance?" Queen Owen's eyebrows furrowed, while Faith's face turned pale.

"This sachet," Timothy said, holding it up, "I found on a servant named Xavier. Surely you recognize it, Queen?"

"Imperial Fragrance?!" Queen Owen gasped. "That's the rare perfume given to me by the Western Regions envoy..." She turned to Faith, enraged. "Faith! How dare you give away my gift to a guard in Hall Zona?!"

Faith fell to her knees with a thud, "Queen, please forgive me! I meant no harm!"

Timothy waved the sachet, "A palace maid of the Central Palace, sneaking off to Hall Zona repeatedly. No wonder you avoided going there on the day I arrived, pushing the food box to me instead. What were you really doing outside Hall Zona alone?"

Terrified, Faith kowtowed, "Queen, have mercy! I swear, I hold no ill intentions towards you! If I lie, may heaven strike me down!"

Everyone knew that a palace maid in Queen Owen's service had once conspired with a guard to strangle her in her sleep, framing it as a sudden illness. The plot was foiled, and Queen Owen ordered the conspirators to be executed.

Since then, Queen Owen had been highly suspicious of her servants mingling with those in Hall Zona. Any found doing so faced severe punishment, ranging from exile to death.

Queen Owen's hand trembled with fury as she pointed at Faith, unable to speak. Her mind was filled with the terrifying memory of nearly being strangled in her sleep.

In the end, Queen Owen stormed out in a rage.

Faith, having failed to expose Timothy and instead incriminating herself, was imprisoned the next day. The servant Xavier disappeared, never to be heard from again.

Despite this, Queen Owen's suspicion of Timothy remained. She ordered him to be watched constantly, monitoring his every move.

She also began distancing herself from Kalle, suspecting that if Timothy had ulterior motives, Kalle might be involved. Kalle, however, was unconcerned. Free from the Queen's service, he enjoyed his time as a study companion in the Eastern Palace. Timothy, too, maintained his usual routine, though he no longer met Christopher in private.

One day, Queen Owen summoned Timothy.

"Supervising the military in Sunder?" Timothy's eyes widened.

"Yes," Queen Owen said, fanning herself and watching his reaction closely. "Sunder, under the jurisdiction of the King of Nixie, has been plagued by disasters and unrest. The King of Nixie has repeatedly requested assistance. Timothy, you are clever and resourceful but lack field experience. This assignment is an opportunity to gain experience and achieve military success. Surely you won't refuse such a golden opportunity?"

Timothy instantly grasped her intention. She was testing him. If he refused to leave the capital, it would suggest he had something to hide regarding Christopher.

Without hesitation, Timothy knelt before Queen Owen, tears in his eyes. "Queen, your trust in me is overwhelming. I will go to Sunder and not disappoint you. I will give my all for the Great Alvah Kingdom!"

Queen Owen was taken aback by his response but quickly smiled, helping him up. "Very well. I am pleased you understand my intentions."

Timothy stood, eager and excited. "When can I depart? Tomorrow? Or the day after?"

Queen Owen laughed, "Such enthusiasm! Don't worry. I've already arranged everything. You will leave in three days."

"Thank you, Queen!" Timothy knelt again, bowing deeply.

Queen Owen watched him, her doubts about Timothy completely dispelled.

In fact, much earlier, she had conducted a similar test on Christopher. When she informed him of Timothy being sent to supervise the military in Sunder, Christopher merely responded with a curt, "Oh."

"Aren't you curious why?" Queen Owen fixed her gaze on Christopher's eyes.

"Do I need to question every decision you make?" Christopher's expression remained utterly unmoved, devoid of any hint of sorrow or joy, as if they were discussing the most mundane of topics. Christopher left it at that and quietly turned away.

On the day Timothy was to depart, Crown Prince Vera and his close friends came to see him off, escorting him all the way to the city gates.

"Timothy, when will you return?" Blake asked.

"Three months," Timothy replied. "It's the Queen's decree."

"Three months?" Vera clutched Timothy's hand forlornly. "That's so long. The thought of not seeing you for three months is unbearable."

Timothy smiled, "Crown Prince, you still have Blake, Arya, and Kalle."

"They are them, you are you. It's not the same!" Vera pouted.

"But Crown Prince, once I leave, you must be careful and protect yourself," Timothy said, squeezing Vera's hand and patting it meaningfully.

"There's something in your words... Timothy, have you heard something?" Blake leaned in, curious.

"Just a hunch. But don't underestimate my intuition; it's usually spot on." Timothy lowered his voice, whispering in Blake's ear, "I have a feeling that within three months, there will be significant changes in the court."

Blake's eyes widened, "If that's true, we must prepare. But with Arya and me here, the Crown Prince will be safe. Don't worry."

Timothy affectionately patted Blake on the shoulder, "I believe in you, brother!"

Arya shot a cold glance their way.

Timothy quickly released Blake and smiled apologetically, "Of course, Arya too!"

"Hmph!" Arya snorted, rolling his eyes.

"Timothy..." Kalle stood to the side, his eyes red and swollen. He quietly hooked his finger around Timothy's, "Remember to write us letters from time to time."

Timothy chuckled, "Oh, our little Kalle can write now? I'm so touched!"

Kalle's lip quivered, and he burst into tears, throwing himself into Timothy's arms, "I learned it for you! Now, just when I'm getting good at it, you leave for three months! Men's words are all lies! I'll never believe you again!"

Timothy awkwardly patted Kalle's back. Vera and Blake exchanged glances and burst into laughter. Even Arya, who had been stone-faced, couldn't help but smile.

After bidding his friends farewell, Timothy set off on his journey alone, riding out of the city.

Reflecting on his time in the palace, Timothy realized how much had happened—too much, really. Despite numerous close calls and almost losing his life several times, his wit and a bit of luck always helped him turn danger into opportunity. Rising from an unknown commoner to the highest-ranking official in the Central Palace, and gaining such loyal friends, made the experience worthwhile.

If there was any regret, it was that since that day at Hall Zona, he hadn't seen Christopher again before his departure for Sunder. Christopher...

As Timothy rode leisurely, he reminisced about their times together, a ripple of emotion stirring in his heart.

Leaving Poiema, his biggest concern wasn't Crown Prince Vera, but Christopher. After all, Vera had Blake and Arya by his side, and the loyal, albeit stubborn, virtuous officials of the court. But Christopher... who did he have? Who genuinely cared about his joys and sorrows, willing to risk their life to protect him?

"I only have you, Timothy."

What had Christopher felt when he whispered those words, clutching him tightly?

Turning back to look at the gradually receding palace, Timothy thought about how, to the common people, the palace's residents seemed distant, enjoying unparalleled luxury and beauty. Yet, the grandeur of the palace was nothing more than a gilded cage. If the canaries within could still sing sweetly, who could truly hear Christopher's heart?

With these complex emotions, Timothy slowly left Poiema. Reaching the banks of the Lushwater, he dismounted, tied his horse to a willow tree, and washed his face in the cold, clear water.

As the ripples on the water's surface settled, they reflected a familiar silhouette. Startled, Timothy looked up abruptly to see a dark figure turning and hurrying away on the bridge.

"Christopher..."

Timothy jumped up, rushing toward the direction of the disappearing figure.

"Christopher! Wait!"

He pushed through the crowd, eyes fixed on the elusive figure. He was certain it was Christopher.

It was the fifth day of the month, the only day Christopher left the palace for meditation.

Timothy chased with renewed determination, heart pounding.

He caught up in a field of wheat, the figure almost within reach. With a leap, Timothy tackled him, and they tumbled together in the green field.

"I've caught you, Your Majesty!"

Timothy clutched the man's waist, looking down at his face—it was indeed Christopher.

"You've lost weight..." Timothy gently touched Christopher's cheek, speaking softly.

Christopher's eyelids fluttered, "It's all your fault."

Timothy kissed the beauty mark at the corner of his eye, "I had no choice but to protect you."

That day, after Faith overheard their conversation and hurried away, Timothy immediately stood up and warned Christopher. Christopher, alarmed, asked how Timothy knew. Timothy explained he had noticed a peculiar fragrance on a servant named Xavier and uncovered his affair with Faith.

The rest was simple: they allowed Faith and Queen Owen to fall into their trap.

Timothy had even anticipated Queen Owen's plan to send him away. He advised Christopher to feign indifference to anything Queen Owen said about him, thus dispelling her suspicions and ensuring their safety.

"Everything in moderation. Queen Owen's arrogance will lead to her downfall. Until then, Your Majesty must endure and, most importantly..."

Timothy looked into Christopher's eyes, "Protect yourself until I return."

Christopher, tears brimming, nodded, "I promise."

Timothy smiled, pulling something from his robe, "Before I leave, I have a gift for you."

Christopher's face darkened, "I don't want any gifts."

"Don't say that. How can you know you won't like it if you don't see it?"

"Do I need to see it? Even if you gave me mountains of gold, it wouldn't compare to having you by my side."

"Oh? So you don't need this lifelike, realistic toy?" Timothy held up a five-inch phallic-shaped object.

Christopher's eyes widened, filled with embarrassment and curiosity, "Where did you get that? And you brought it along?"

"Don't mind the details." Timothy pulled Christopher's hand, placing the toy in his palm, whispering, "Feel it. It's incredible. It looks hard but is soft to the touch, like real skin. If you soak it in warm water, it expands. Imagine putting this inside you—how delightful that would be?"

Christopher blushed deeply, holding the toy in his hand and curiously squeezing it. He couldn't help but marvel, "The world is full of wonders. I had no idea such things existed; I've never even heard of this in the palace."

Timothy chuckled, "Well, what do you think? With this, if you feel lonely at night, you can use it and pretend it's me. I guarantee it will make you feel ecstasy every night. Time will fly by, and three months will pass in no time."

Christopher, hearing this, couldn't help but laugh despite himself, "You scoundrel, who compares themselves to a toy? Can't you wish for something better?"

"What's wrong with that?" Timothy replied, unabashed. "Desire is natural. Have you forgotten how we met? Do you need me to remind you?"

As he spoke, Timothy slid his hand into Christopher's robe, rubbing the desire between his legs through the fabric.

Christopher moaned softly, writhing with discomfort, "You... you're not planning to do it here, are you?"

Timothy swiftly pulled down Christopher's pants, laughing seductively, "Did you chase me here just to say goodbye? Didn't you think of doing something else?"

Christopher, unlike Timothy, was not so bold. Even if he had thought about it, he would never admit it. His face turned away in embarrassment, yet his legs spread involuntarily in a gesture of consent.

"No one will see us here, will they?" Christopher asked nervously.

"Even if they do, they wouldn't recognize us." Timothy spat into his hand, spreading the saliva over Christopher's entrance. "Here, you don't have to worry about anyone's eyes. You can cry out as loud as you want."

Encouraged by Timothy's words, Christopher's pent-up frustration and longing exploded. He embraced Timothy passionately, their lips locking in a deep kiss.

After a long, passionate kiss, Christopher eagerly lay down, wrapping his legs around Timothy's waist.

"Don't be so hasty, Your Majesty. Let's try this toy first." Timothy pressed the toy against Christopher's entrance, slowly working it in. "How does it feel, Your Majesty?"

Christopher's abdomen convulsed, and he moaned, "So big... so thick..."

"It will get even bigger, Your Majesty." Timothy twisted the toy inside Christopher's hole, hitting the most sensitive spot. Meanwhile, he freed his own erection, stroking it as he watched the toy move in and out.

"It really is getting bigger..." Christopher moaned, his tight hole gripping the toy as it thrust in and out. "It's so full..."

"Forgive me, Your Majesty!" Timothy turned, presenting his hard member to Christopher's face. Consumed by desire, Christopher instinctively licked the tip, tasting the salty pre-cum before taking it into his mouth.

Timothy didn't waste any time. He began sucking on Christopher's smaller member while thrusting the toy deeper into his hole. Christopher's body trembled, overwhelmed by the dual sensations, his moans muffled by Timothy's cock in his mouth.

As the warm breeze rustled the wheat, their entwined bodies were partially hidden. Without Christopher's cries, no one would have known what they were doing in the field.

"Right there... I can't take it... Ah!" Christopher's voice cracked, his body spasming. Timothy's cock thrust deeper into his throat, silencing him.

Seeing Christopher's reaction, Timothy knew he had hit the right spot. He sucked harder, causing Christopher's body to jerk violently, reaching a non-ejaculatory climax.

With Christopher satiated, it was Timothy's turn. He flipped Christopher over, positioning himself against the toy still lodged in his hole.

"Your Majesty, I'm coming in," Timothy said.

Christopher swallowed nervously, then spread his cheeks with his hands, exposing his quivering hole. "Do it... quickly..."

Timothy's breath hitched at the sight. He aligned his cock and pushed in beside the toy.

"Ah!" Christopher felt like he was being torn apart, his hole stretched to its limit by both the toy and Timothy. Timothy pressed his chest to Christopher's back, their lips meeting in another deep kiss. As Timothy moved deeper, their lips parted, both gasping for air.

Once fully inside, Timothy waited for Christopher to adjust before moving.

When Christopher finally relaxed, Timothy began thrusting gently. Their lips parted, and Christopher, exhausted, could only kneel, his ass raised for Timothy. The sound of their bodies colliding grew louder as Timothy picked up the pace, the toy and his cock working in tandem.

"I can't bear to leave you, Your Majesty..." Timothy said, licking his lips as he thrust harder.

"Timothy... don't go..." Christopher's voice was broken by sobs, unsure if he cried from the pleasure or the impending separation. Seeing Christopher like this, Timothy's heart ached. He wished he could stay with him always, but reality meant they would soon part. He pushed the thought aside, focusing on the present moment.

In the vast field, the only sounds were their heavy breathing and Christopher's moans, creating a symphony of farewell pleasure.

About the Author

Shuang Chenyue, a renowned author of female-oriented romantic fiction in China, was born in Nanning, Guangxi. After graduating from Sichuan International Studies University, she pursued her graduate studies in Japan at Doshisha University's Sociology Department in Kyoto. Upon obtaining her master's degree, she returned to China and currently resides in Shanghai. She is a VIP author on the Haitang Culture online literature platform, specializing in writing romantic fiction with themes such as martial arts, political intrigue, and fantasy, often set in an imaginary ancient China. Her representative works include "Unrecognizable him" and "The Beauty with Poison."

Read more at https://www.missevan.com/sound/3625999.